# Deep Deceit

## Anne Louise O'Connell

*Anne Louise O'Connell*

Cover design by Creation Booth
www.creationbooth.com

DISCLAIMER
All of the characters in this book are fictional. None of them exists in real life.

*Deep Deceit*

*This book is dedicated to all the amazing women I met in Dubai who warmly welcomed me from day one, especially Wendy and Jane, and to my fellow Flamingo Authors and Phuket Writers' Group*

*Anne Louise O'Connell*

# Chapter 1

Sweat mingled with sunscreen and sand, streaming into Susan's eyes, almost blinding her. Her arms shook and she didn't know how much more she could take.

"Come on girls... give me 10 more or no water break!" screamed the burly Neanderthal Susan had nicknamed 'The Sadist'. She looked over at the latest newcomer whose face glowed a brilliant shade of crimson and who, after each push-up, fell flat on her belly, and Susan felt sorry for her. She'd introduce herself and take her for a cold one once this evening's desert boot camp finished.

Susan's shoulders burned from the effort as she struggled to 'give him' two more. Another unchecked grunt burst from between her clenched teeth. The rest of the co-ed class, in various phases of weight-loss and/or bodybuilding obsession, groaned and panted in unison. She snuck another glance at the newbie who returned a wide-eyed, pain-wracked look as she collapsed into the sand again. Susan wondered what could possibly motivate this woman to inflict such pain on herself.

This was Susan's second round at boot camp. The only thing that kept her coming back was that it helped her shed what everyone called the 'Dubai stone', a whopping 14 pounds. She had gained it since moving to the most glamorous place on earth, with lots of temptation and not too much work. After she and her husband had moved to Dubai, she had decided to take a break from the psychiatric nursing she'd been doing for 13 years. She hadn't realized how being on her feet, running from patient to patient, had kept her in shape. She started 'boot camp' after she caught a glimpse of her widening rear-end in a shop window reflecting back at her in all its calorie-induced glory. The testing of new restaurants, Friday all-you-can-eat and drink brunches and the thrice- weekly ladies lunches had caught up with her. She swore once she dropped the extra weight, which showed dramatically on her petite frame, she would be more careful in the future.

"Okay folks... great work," the Sadist admitted. "See you next week!"

Susan cracked open her bottle of lukewarm water and poured half of it over her head, then downed the rest like a crazed, water deprived person lost in the desert.

"I don't think I'll be back next week. I'm not cut out for this," the newbie walked up to Susan and put out her hand. "You were awesome... I'd really like to shake your hand because it looks like you're a pro."

"Aw, thanks. I sure wasn't a pro a few months ago but I can do it now without too much pain... I'm Susan," she said shaking the outstretched hand that was offered.

"Celeste," she puffed. "Sorry, haven't quite caught my breath yet." Celeste bent down with her hands on her knees.

Susan laughed. "He is a bit of a task master." She lowered her voice. "I actually call him the Sadist. But I promise it does get easier."

Celeste nodded and smiled. "It's really nice to meet you. I don't know many people here yet and I thought this would be a good place to make new friends." She brushed the sand off her front and tried to smooth down her hair. "It'll have to be someone who isn't into looks, that's for sure!"

"Well, I'd love to buy you a drink if you've got time... nothing like a cold beer to reward yourself for surviving a work out with Ivan." Susan tilted her head towards their instructor and grimaced.

"Actually, I'd like that. My husband's away and my daughter is sleeping over at a friend's so I'm pretty free and easy."

"Great, there's a place called Long's Bar not far from here," Susan offered. "It'll still be happy hour and they've got great pub grub. And, some of the football clubs go there after their games so we can go as we are! We won't be nearly as smelly as them!"

"Okay, sounds perfect," Celeste stomped her feet to get the sand off as they stepped from the beach onto the sidewalk. "Can I follow you? I don't know my way around yet and even though I've lived all over the world I'm finding it's probably the most difficult place I've had to navigate."

"I felt the same way when we arrived a year ago and I still get lost sometimes. Everyone complains about it but they all say it's much better than it used to be... it wasn't long ago that they didn't even have street names," Susan rolled her eyes. "It's not far so why don't you ride with me and I'll bring you back to your car when we're done. I'm right here," Susan pointed to a red Jeep Wrangler with the top off and vaulted into the driver's seat.

Celeste looked forlornly at Susan. "I'm afraid I'm not quite as nimble as you... I've got a few extra pounds."

"Don't be silly, you're fine... and, there is a door you can use. Mine's just broken and I haven't had the time to get it fixed. Here..." Susan leaned over and pushed the passenger door open. "Seems I'm busier now than when I was working 12-hour shifts!"

"Thanks." Celeste climbed in. "Twelve-hour shifts? What do you do?"

"Actually, I'm a nurse but I decided to take a break when we moved here. I'd been working in a psych ward of a hospital in New Jersey and it was pretty stressful." Susan shifted the Jeep into first gear and pulled away from the curb. "I know she rides a little rough and it's kind of windy but I've wanted one of these since I was in college."

"At least we don't have to worry about messing our hair," Celeste laughed. "Mine's already a disaster anyway."

Susan turned onto Sheikh Zayed Road, the main thoroughfare that ran north-south connecting two of the seven United Arab Emirates, Dubai and Abu Dhabi. It was a highway that inspired hair-raising stories around the world, with the YouTube videos to prove it.

The wind buffeted their voices so they lapsed into a companionable silence for the short ride. Susan took the next ramp and was soon pulling in front of the Towers Rotana Hotel.

"Is it in the hotel?" asked Celeste.

"Yeah, it's in the basement. All the bars here are located in hotels because of the crazy laws around serving and even drinking alcohol." Susan grabbed a ball cap from the floor of the back seat and stuffed her hair up into it. One black curl escaped under the brim and she brushed it back over her ear. "Do you have your alcoholics drinks license yet?"

"My what?"

"How long did you say you've been here? That was the first thing my husband did... well, as soon as we had our residency stuff sorted out." Susan linked her arm into Celeste's and guided her up the stairs and into the lobby.

"Just a couple of months but I only have a tourist visa so far. My husband is working in Saudi and he's supposed to be coming back next week to take care of all the paperwork." Celeste's voice cracked and Susan thought her new friend was about to cry.

"Well, now you've got me and I'm happy to help. Don't worry… it'll all come together, you'll see. We were really lucky. My husband is a pilot for Emirates and they took care of all that for us. I can just imagine what it's like to have to do it all by yourself. Now that I think of it, you *really* need that drink!"

Celeste was so relieved she finally had a friend she could talk to. The first couple of months had been a whirlwind of packing and moving, finding temporary accommodation, getting her daughter Tamara registered for school, organizing all the documentation that would be needed when her husband, Ryan, finally joined them. No matter how many times she had moved since becoming an expat, it didn't seem to get any easier. They had spent several years in Africa and the last two in Saudi. Even though they had made some wonderful friends and the compound they lived in had everything they needed, Tamara was starting to baulk at the oppressive nature of the Saudi laws. Not being able to go out of the compound without being covered from head to toe, with only her face showing, was getting frustrating for her.

Celeste followed Susan into the bar and they picked a table in the corner, away from the enthusiastic, beer-drinking, dart throwing footballers, so they could chat. Susan waved and held up two fingers at a waitress who was carrying a tray of draft beer.

"You don't know how nice it is to finally have someone to talk to," Celeste put her hand on Susan's arm. "I've been so busy getting Tamara settled. It's been particularly difficult for her... as a teenager it's tough to change schools and it's her last year of high school. I'm so focused on her transition I haven't had time to do anything for myself, which I know is important but there are only so many hours in a day," Celeste sighed. "Do you have any children?"

"No, Mitch and I... that's my husband... well, we decided that we weren't going to have kids. We both had full time jobs we loved and I just couldn't see bringing a kid into this world..." Susan's voice trailed off. "Mmm... sorry. I don't mean to be negative... and someone's got to populate the earth, right?" Susan clinked Celeste's glass.

"It's okay... I only have one for pretty much the same reason. Every day I'm panic-stricken watching Tamara walk out the door, not knowing what might happen. I wish I could put her in bubble wrap and glue myself to her." Celeste took a long guzzle of her beer. "We've lived in Africa and Saudi and now I can't get out of the habit of making sure she's not going anywhere alone. She thinks I'm paranoid."

Susan laughed. "Well, here's to safety in numbers," she raised her glass and they toasted again.

"Amen!" Celeste relaxed and the two women fell into a comfortable repartee, sharing stories and getting to know one another.

"Oh wow... look at the time," Celeste held up her watch. "It's after midnight and I've got a realtor coming bright and early to take me to see a few places. Do you mind if we call it a night?"

Celeste was thoroughly enjoying the conversation but she would need her sleep if she was going to get through the next day. She hated house hunting, especially without Ryan but he was expecting her to have a place picked out by the time he arrived.

"No problem." Susan waved the waitress down and asked for the check. "Where are you thinking of living?"

"I honestly don't know." Celeste put some money down on the table and Susan slid it back to her.

"My treat... you can get the next one."

"Thanks, that's really sweet of you." Celeste put the bills back in her purse. "We're living in a temporary hotel apartment in *Al Barsha* until our shipment arrives. I'm supposed to be looking at places in The Springs and Meadows tomorrow."

"Well, if I can help, let me know. Here's my number." Susan jotted her cell phone number on a napkin and gave it to Celeste.

Celeste carefully folded it like it was a treasure and slid it into the side pocket of her purse. "Thanks. You can be sure I will be taking advantage of that."

### Deep Deceit

"Anytime! Come on... I'll take you to your car so you can get home and get your beauty sleep."

## *Chapter 2*

The alarm shrilled at 7:00 a.m. and Celeste groggily rolled over to hit the snooze. She groaned as the pain shot down her arm as she attempted to lift it, desperate to silence the incessant ringing. She felt like she had been hit by a bus, dragged across an intersection and dumped by the roadside like disposable road kill. Her arm fell onto the top of her clock/radio and she curled back into a fetal position, whimpering and recalling the apt nickname Susan had given the beach combat instructor. He really was a sadist if he knew how much pain his class would be in the next day... or maybe it was just her.

She sat up slowly, taking inventory of her body parts that hollered at her to be careful, then gingerly slid her legs off the side of the bed, placed her feet on the floor, gently applied pressure and stood up. Her calf muscles screamed in agony as she limped to the bathroom, her lower back twanging at each and every step. Her thighs argued painfully as she lowered herself onto the toilet. Her butt cheeks wouldn't accept the pressure so she suffered the burning in her thighs as she tried to pee.

*Jesus... is there anything that I didn't pull or strain?* Celeste struggled back to bed saying a silent prayer of thanks that she wouldn't have to deal with getting Tamara out of bed and off to school. She reached for her phone and scrolled through her contacts to find Kim the realtor's number.

There was no way she could traipse all over town looking at the 10-plus apartments, houses and villas she had lined up. Celeste almost started to cry thinking about walking up any stairs and the inevitable construction debris she'd have to navigate around. She stopped as she was about to hit 'dial' and realized she had no choice. Ryan would be back in five days and this was the only day Kim would be available. Celeste had already seen a slew of places and had one in mind that she thought would work but she needed to be sure... needed to be able to tell Ryan that she had seen every possible option available before making her decision. She cringed as she recalled his exact instructions as they said good-bye at the airport in Riyadh and she was suggesting they wait until he got to Dubai to find a place. "Just *pick* one for Christ sake. I won't have time to fuck around when I get there."

With his words still ringing in her ears, Celeste dragged herself out of bed again and into the bathroom to run a hot bath. She knew whatever she chose wouldn't suit him. It seemed she couldn't do anything right lately. If she picked a villa, he'd probably say he would have preferred an apartment and vice versa. Tamara hadn't been much help as she was too busy with her new friends to even come see any of the places. Since it was Friday, the first day of the weekend in the UAE, Celeste had insisted that Tamara join her for the last round so she could have some input and not complain. Celeste knew she would have to meticulously weigh the pros and cons to explain to Ryan when she presented him with her choice and it would be helpful to have Tamara on her side. He seemed to value her opinion more than his wife's lately.

Ryan would only be back for a few days this time to get her and Tamara's residence visas sorted out and then he had to return to Saudi. He was a contractor, owned his own company and the project he was working on was behind schedule. He felt immense pressure to get it done. But it seemed like every time he made progress some prince or sheikh decided that the windows weren't big enough or the pillars didn't look grand enough or that a whole new wing needed to be added or something even crazier. It was some showcase government building but Celeste didn't know the details. Ryan was pretty secretive about it all.

It would probably be good to be apart from each other for a while as he continued to work on his project in Saudi. He planned to spend a week every two months with her and Tamara in Dubai. At least that was what he had proposed but he was at the whim of his client, in effect, the Royal family.

### *Deep Deceit*

She cranked up the A/C for a little relief from the sweltering 40 degrees Celsius outside. It may have seemed crazy to get into a tub full of hot water but it would help ease her muscle pain. She added some rose hip bubble bath under the cascading water and followed it into the tub, sinking under the white fluffy mountains with a sigh. She deeply inhaled the relaxing floral scent. Maybe she should try yoga instead of boot camp.

Tamara jammed her t-shirt into her overnight bag and ran her fingers through her hair.

"So there's a bunch of us headed to the mall this afternoon... probably gonna go skiing if it's not too crowded," Tamara's new friend and classmate, Heidi handed a brush to her. "It's too hot to go to the beach... I can't believe it's already so hot and it's only May," Heidi pouted.

"Well, it can't be any hotter than Saudi but I mostly stayed inside in the air con anyway." Tamara ran the brush roughly through her hair and pulled it up in a ponytail. She took the long blond strands out of the hairbrush and dropped them in the wastebasket under Heidi's desk. "I wish I could go with you but I promised my mom I'd go house-hunting with her... she's so useless, she can't go by herself."

"Just call her and tell her something came up and you can't go with," Heidi crossed her arms.

"Nah... she'd have a fit. My dad's coming in a few days and we're supposed to have a place picked out. She says she needs my input... and she's going to pick me up soon anyways." Right on cue a car horn sounded outside.

"Tamara, your mom's here," Heidi's mom called up the stairs.

"Guess I gotta go but I'll try to catch up with you later."

"Yeah sure... just call me on my mobile."

The girls bounded down the stairs. "Thanks Mrs. Fletcher." Tamara opened the front door and the blast of heat slapped her in the face like the back draft of a 747. She shaded her eyes with her hand blocking the bits of sand the wind had collected and was tossing about.

"You're welcome dear, come back any time." Heidi's mom waved out the door at Celeste. "Looks like we've got a *shamal* brewing... the dust is really kicking up. Better get in the car quick or you'll get sand blasted."

Tamara ran to the car and slammed the door, closing out the suffocating heat and stinging nettles of sand that chased her and swirled around her head and between her legs.

"This is going to be fun," she snapped on her seatbelt, crossed her arms and stared forward.

"I know... I'm sorry but I can't cancel," soothed Celeste. "This is the last chance we'll have to see a few more places so we can make a decision before your dad gets here."

"I know... whatever."

18

"So, how was your slumber party?" Celeste patted Tamara's knee.

"Oh for crying out loud mom... I just stayed with a friend.  I'm not six years old you know." Tamara brushed her mother's hand away and dug in her purse for her iPhone and tore at the headset that was tangled together. "Jesus, these things are so fucking messed up!"

"Tamara, please don't swear.  I've told you a hundred times, I don't like it."

"Well, dad does all the time... it's no big deal."

Celeste chose to let it go. It wasn't worth fighting about and they always seemed to be at odds lately. She also decided to ignore the faint smell of stale beer. Tamara was 18 so Celeste was sure she had the occasional drink. It wasn't uncommon among teens everywhere but the expat communities seemed to be worse.

"So, did you have a nice time? What's Heidi like? I wish I had had time to go in and say hello. I hope they understood... you did tell them why we were in a bit of a rush, didn't you?"

Tamara rolled her eyes and finally got her head phones untangled, stuck them in her ears and turned away.

*Oh joy... this is going to be a long day.* Celeste reached up and switched on the GPS.

As Celeste suspected, the day was agonizing. Her feet and legs ached, Tamara pouted the whole time, wanting to be with her friends at the mall, the Filipina realtor chatted on her mobile phone all day and when Celeste tried to ask a question, glared at her and put her hand impatiently on her hip to answer... with an incomplete or irrelevant bit of information.

"You want this one? I can do paperwork now," was her constant chant throughout the exhausting day.

At the sixth stop, Celeste had finally had enough and pulled Tamara aside.

"Okay, I can't keep them all straight anymore so let's pick one and call it a day... what do you think?"

"I think we should take this one... it has big bedrooms and a pool."

"Well, it's a little more than we were budgeting for but it is close to your school so we'll save on gas. And, it's away from the busyness of downtown and very peaceful. Maybe I can start writing again." Celeste thought about the three unfinished novels that languished on her hard drive all set in Africa with romance and intrigue dying to make their debut.

"Mmmm... can we go now? I don't want to miss my friends."

So, that was it. Celeste told the realtor to start the ball rolling and that her husband would be back soon to finalize all the necessary paperwork. They were going to live in The Springs.

As they exited onto the pulse-raising, gasp-inducing, 12-lane speedway of Sheikh Zayed Road, Celeste was too relieved at making a decision about where they would live to be bothered by the imposing SUVs that whizzed by. She happily stayed in the center lane, which she had gotten used to so the maniacs could just go around her. Everyone was obviously in more of a hurry than she was and oh so much more important.

Tamara had resumed her sulking position in the corner with ear-buds firmly in place so Celeste resigned herself to humming along to the radio. A casual glance to her rearview mirror brought her out of her reverie as a huge white SUV bore down on her. Her reflexes told her to change lanes to get out of his way and she quickly checked over her shoulder and veered into the right lane as the driver tailgating her did the same.

"Mom! What the hell are you doing?" Tamara sat up as the swift motion jammed her into her door.

"I'm trying to get away from this lunatic... he's riding my bumper!"

The white Escalade continued to tailgate Celeste and flashed his lights at her.

"He won't even let me get out of his way... he keeps changing lanes right along with me." Celeste's voice rose in a panic.

"It's a local too," sneered Tamara. "What an asshole!"

"No it's not... check out the license plate," Celeste gripped the steering wheel trying to maintain control as she sped up in an attempt to pull away. "They're Saudi plates. See? Tamara, try to get a plate number okay? I'm going to report this guy."

Celeste maneuvered her way over to the exit hoping her 'tail' would be headed towards downtown and keep going. The Escalade crossed over the three lanes behind her and continued flashing his lights.

"Mom... he's still following us and he looks really mad. What's up his ass?"

"I guess he thinks I cut him off back there."

Celeste's right tire caught the edge of the exit lane asphalt and she almost lost control. She swerved back into the lane and just as she corrected her course she felt a bump from behind.

"Holy shit, he's ramming us!"

"Tamara, call the police... you've got the number programmed in your phone. I'm going to try to get off this exit and pull into a gas station or something." Celeste was surprised how calm her voice sounded as her stomach was doing flip-flops and her heart had lodged itself right under her chin.

The next ramming from behind sent Celeste off the road, onto the shoulder and into the soft sand where she skidded and came to a halt with the Escalade still in pursuit. She floored the accelerator and the tires spun wildly, burying the little rental car's tires deep into the sand on the shoulder. Celeste could hear Tamara desperately trying to explain what was happening to the switchboard operator at the police station, who most likely didn't speak English.

"Mom, he's out of his car and he's coming this way!"

Celeste watched helplessly as a tall, ghost-like apparition in a flowing white *dishdisha* and a red and white checked head covering bore down on her as she frantically locked the doors.

"Have you gotten through to anyone yet?" Celeste's voice cracked and her throat tightened like someone's hands were already wrapped around it.

"This is ridiculous mom... we didn't do anything... he's just a big bully." Tamara reached for her door handle ready to get out.

"Tamara NO!" Celeste grabbed her arm and yanked her back. "He's not going to listen to reason, especially not from a lippy teenager." Celeste could feel the anxiety rising and took several deep breaths. "We'll just wait for the police."

The man came up from behind the car and hammered his fist on the roof. "Get out, get out!" He yelled, his face flushed a brilliant red, matching his headscarf.

"Tamara don't look at him. Just keep looking ahead."

They could hear a police siren and Celeste prayed that it was coming in their direction. Surely the cop would see the situation and pull over.

She stole a glance in the rearview mirror and saw her prayers had been answered. The hammering stopped as the policeman pulled over and got out of his vehicle. Celeste's mouth dropped open as she watched the two men approach each other and then shake hands.

Celeste slowly opened the car door and stepped out onto the sand. She started advancing towards the policeman and he looked at her sternly and held up his hand. She stopped and leaned on the hatch back. Tamara came charging out of the passenger side, shaking with rage and pointing her finger. "That asshole tried to run us off the road!"

Celeste sidestepped into Tamara's path, ignoring the jabbing pain in her leg muscles and blocked her advance. She grabbed both her daughter's shoulders and forced her to look in her eyes. She leaned close and hissed into her ear, "That can get you arrested here. Don't forget... you've lived in this part of the world long enough to know better." Celeste loosened her grip as she watched Tamara's rage melt into fear. "Now, get back in the car and stay there. I'll handle this," she said and gently turned her towards the passenger side door.

Celeste put on her very bravest front and a conciliatory smile and started to walk towards the men again. "Officer, if I could please tell you what happened, I'm sure we can work this all out," she began.

The officer took two steps towards her, his hand on his hip holster, growled something in Arabic and said one word, "License," and held out his hand. Celeste handed it to him and he waved at her, dismissing her. He turned back to his conversation with the Saudi who was jabbering away, waving his arms agitatedly, pointing and gesturing from the highway and back to Celeste, glowering at her.

Celeste backed off knowing better than to argue but searched her mind wildly for a solution. She took her phone out of her pocket and dialed the only friend she had. She listened to it ring at the other end and crossed her fingers that Susan would answer.

"Hello?"

"Oh, thank God you're home... Susan, it's Celeste."

"Oh... Hi Celeste, nice to hear from you so soon. Is everything okay? You sound out of breath."

"I've just had an accident and the police are here and I didn't know who else to call..." her voice trailed off.

"Wow... that's too bad... do you want me to come? Are you okay? Is your daughter with you?"

"Yes, she is and we're both okay. I'm so sorry to bother you but I just thought someone should know because I've got a bad feeling about this." Celeste looked around her and realized she didn't even know where she was. She had just taken the first exit she saw and didn't remember seeing a sign and her surroundings weren't familiar.

"Why the bad feeling?" Susan cut into Celeste's thoughts.

"Well, I was basically run off the road by a big SUV with Saudi plates and now the guy's talking to the police and they won't let me tell my side... gosh, I don't even know if they speak English! What am I going to do?" The tears started welling up in her eyes.

"Don't worry, I'm sure he'll get your story too. Just make sure you get a copy of the report in case you have to make an insurance claim... and, if it wasn't your fault, get the green copy not the red one."

"It definitely wasn't my fault... he sped up from behind and was flashing his lights at me. I changed lanes to get out of his way and he changed at the same time so he probably thinks I cut him off." Celeste wiped her sweaty palms on her slacks and brushed a long strand of hair out of her eyes. "Then he rammed into me and kept following and ran me onto the shoulder. I'm totally mired down in the sand. I think I'm going to need a tow truck."

"Do you want me to come?"

"No, I can't even begin to explain our location. I'll just get the report and wait for a tow. Hopefully the police officer will be able to tell the towing company where we are. I'll call you later and let you know how it goes. Thanks for listening."

"Sure. Just call me if you need me for anything."

"I will, thanks." Celeste hung up and got into the air-conditioned car.

"What's happening?" Tamara craned her neck around to look out the back window.

"I'm not sure but I just called my friend Susan and she said to make sure to get the green report." She sighed and dug a scrunchie out of her purse and stuck her hair in a ponytail.

"Aw mom... those are so not cool!"

"I think we have more to worry about than my lack of fashion sense Tamara." Celeste reached over to the glove box to get the rental agreement and dialed the company. "Hopefully they'll be able to sort out a tow truck for us while we're waiting."

"Mom, the cop is standing at the window."

Celeste rolled the window down as his close proximity made it impossible for her to open the door. He handed her the report. "Your copy for insurance." He snipped and turned away.

"Sir, wait!" Celeste called after him confused, looking at the red sheet of paper he had handed her. She got out of her car just as the Escalade pulled away. The driver sneered at her as he drove by and gunned the engine, disappearing at the bottom of the ramp.

She followed the police officer and watched him retrieve a clipboard from the roof. He pulled her license from the clip and handed it back to her.

"Why did I get the red copy?" Celeste held the sheet up and rattled it at him.

"Yes, you get red copy for insurance." He waved at her again and got into his car and closed the door shutting out any further argument. He drove away leaving Celeste agape, hands on her hips.

She slowly walked back to the car and got in.

"Well?" Tamara plucked a non-existent piece of lint off her skirt.

"I got the red..."

"So glad you took care of that," Tamara practically snorted at her. "Maybe I should just flag a taxi. Hopefully I can still catch Heidi at the mall."

Before Celeste could gather her thoughts, Tamara had walked to the edge of the road and successfully flagged a cab. Celeste watched as the taxi faded into the distance.

# Chapter 3

Celeste poured herself a shot of whiskey. It wasn't her favorite but it was all she had handy. She had bought it for when Ryan came back and she needed something strong to calm her still shaking nerves. The rental company had sent a tow truck after Celeste described her surroundings as best she could. She was amazed the driver found her and then the tow truck driver told her there was a 'LoJack' vehicle recovery system built into the GPS so they were able to pinpoint her exact location, which they hadn't mentioned during the conversation. It certainly would have saved her a lot of angst! He had dropped her at the hotel/apartment and the rental company was going to bring her another car in the morning. *I sure won't be driving anywhere tonight!*

Tamara could take a damn taxi home she thought as she downed her drink. It burned on the way down but the warm glow that followed immediately behind was the result she was looking for. The tears came next as a feeling of abject loneliness overtook her like a creeping vine over a Transylvanian castle wall. What was up with Tamara lately? They used to talk and hang out and now she was like a different person. And, she sure couldn't talk to Ryan. He would tell her to grow up and stop acting like a child. Things had been different between them since they'd moved to Saudi three years ago and she couldn't put her finger on it. He was hiding something. She was sure of that. But, they were good at concealing their feelings from each other and had kept up quite a façade since they married almost 19 years ago... very soon after Donald, Celeste's first husband and Ryan's business partner, had died.

They had been working on a project in Nigeria when Donald went missing. They feared a kidnapping and were expecting a ransom note or call to demand money. Other wealthy businessmen had been taken and released after their companies or families put up millions of dollars so it had triggered an underground movement of kidnappers, some more ruthless than others. The call never came and neither did the note. Less than a month after he went missing, Donald's body was found dumped in a ditch on the side of the road in Lagos. The police report said it was a mugging.

Celeste was numb and Ryan never left her side. She had relied on Donald for everything. She felt abandoned, alone and afraid in a foreign country. She had no family to speak of except her aunt who lived in North Dakota. Her parents died in a car accident a few years before so she was totally alone. She had clung to Ryan in desperation, his burly body a protective shield, so warm and strong and virile. Celeste had given in to the desire before Donald's body had even been found and 19 years later, she was still wracked with guilt.

At the funeral Celeste gripped Ryan's hand like the last spike on the side of a mountain. His marriage proposal a week later seemed cold and callous but Celeste accepted, not knowing what else to do. She had no where to go and Donald's will left his half of the company to her so, in an exhaustion-fueled haze, Ryan had convinced her it was what Donald would have wanted.

After the pain faded and her head cleared, she realized Ryan had taken advantage of her vulnerability and she wondered if she had made a huge mistake. But she didn't feel there was any other option so she decided to stick it out... especially with a baby on the way.

"Hey Mitch, remember the gal I told you about who I met at beach combat?" Susan stirred the pasta while her husband chopped the garlic and tomatoes to put in the spaghetti sauce.

"Sure... what about her?"

"Well, she had a really bad experience on Sheikh Zayed Road today and I'm wondering if I should call and invite her over." Susan refilled her wine glass and took a sip.

"If you want to, we've got plenty here." Mitch leaned over and kissed her on the forehead.

"Yeah, I think I'll at least call to check on her. She didn't get back to me so I assume everything is okay... but her husband's away and she doesn't really know anyone here yet."

"Okay Ms. Fixer-upper... go give her a call so you can stop worrying," Mitch gave her a pat on the bum. "I'll put the rest of the stuff in the sauce and then leave it to simmer."

Susan adored her husband. He was a great cook, a funny guy and amazing in bed. She'd lucked out when she met him. She had just turned 25 and had started working at a private care facility for severely mentally disabled. Mitch's brother was one of her patients. The second she'd laid eyes on Mitch as he'd walked towards the nurses' station she'd fallen madly in love. She became a firm believer in love at first sight. They'd been married now for 10 years and her friends and family never got tired of reminding her what a catch Mitch was. He had his irritating quirks for sure but the good outweighed the bad.

"Thanks... I'll make it quick." She ran into the bedroom, hopped on her bed, crossed her legs lotus-style and dialed her phone.

"Hello?"

"Hey Celeste, it's Susan... I just wanted to call and check in since I hadn't heard back after your crisis call."

"Oh... I'm so sorry Susan... everything's fine and I'm back home. Well, actually not everything." Celeste paused and sighed loudly into Susan's ear.

"Why? What happened? Wait, don't tell me now 'cause I'm calling to invite you over anyway. Mitch has cooked up a storm here and there's way too much for the two of us so why don't you and Tamara come over for dinner and you can tell us all about it over a nice glass of cab sav."

"Mmmmm, that would be terrific..." Celeste's voice cracked. "You don't know how comforting it is to hear a friendly voice and I would love to come for dinner. But it'll be just me... Tamara's at the mall with her friends and I'm sure she's grabbing a bite there."

"Great... it's nothing fancy but I promise it'll be scrumptious. Why don't you grab a cab and then you can have a couple drinks.... Sounds like you need it!"

"Sounds perfect. There are usually a few parked right out front so I should be there in about half an hour. Is that okay?

"Sure. Take your time and we'll see you soon." Susan hung up the phone and padded back into the kitchen, which was her favorite room in the house. It was brightly lit and she and Mitch had painted the walls a soft olive green when they moved in. The entire place had been a boring off-white and, since the house belonged to the company, they would have to return it to its previous drab state but they would be there for a few more years at least so adding a splash of color was worth it.

"Is your friend coming?"

"Ya... she'll be here shortly. She sounded upset." Susan crunched on a raw carrot, her favorite snack food these days.

"Well, I can't imagine any run-in with the local law enforcement is going to be much fun. The upside is that she's not in jail, right?"

They had heard stories about people going to jail for the craziest things, like giving another driver the finger (if the other driver was a local and reported you). One of their friends' sons had even spent a night in jail for public intoxication and underage drinking. His mother had been frantic since the American 'right to a phone call' wasn't part of the drill in Dubai and it wasn't until the next morning that the police called his parents to come get him. Seemed a little harsh to Susan but the experience did teach him a lesson.

"I'm sure getting run off the road wasn't much fun either... I wonder if she got the green copy."

"From the sounds of it she should have but you know how it goes around here sometimes," Mitch handed Susan the salad bowls. "If you don't speak the language, you're never sure what the other guy is saying."

"True," Susan took a sip of her wine and grabbed the bowl. "Even after being here for a couple years it's hard to really understand the intricacies of the place. It's downright baffling. Can't work without my husband's permission; no drinking without a license, multiple wives allowed and no eating or drinking in public for a whole month because of a religious holiday, even though I'm not Muslim. And, there are really no guidelines. There should be a users' guide handed to you on the plane when you first arrive... although that would probably just add to the confusion since the rules seem to change from one day to the next."

# *Chapter 4*

The slamming door woke Celeste out of a dead sleep. She looked over at the clock on her night table and the red luminescent numbers read three-zero-zero. *Shit... it's three in the bloody morning and Tamara is just getting home now?* Celeste had had a lovely evening with Susan and her husband and felt almost happy and semi-normal for a change. It had been a while since she'd spent time with people who were so easy-going and friendly. The expat community in Nigeria had been very cliquey and she never felt like she fit in. It was even worse in Saudi. Her bouts of depression hadn't helped much either.

Rolling over she dragged the covers over her head, not wanting another confrontation with Tamara. Celeste had been tipsy when she got home around midnight and thought for sure her daughter had been tucked into bed and hadn't checked on her. Subconsciously, she knew she should have... as any good mother would. Denial was one of her favorite defense mechanisms. It was a difficult situation. Tamara was 18 and according to the law, an adult, but she was still in school and still Celeste and Ryan's responsibility... although it looked as though Ryan would be a parent in-absentia for most of Tamara's final year in high school. If she was going to set some ground rules it might as well be now.

Celeste exhaled a long reverberating breath and swung her legs off the bed, bracing herself for a battle. She crossed the hallway of their temporary suite and knocked on Tamara's door.

"What?" Tamara's voice grated through the closed door.

"I'm coming in. We need to talk." Celeste said with all the bravado she could muster and entered the room just as Tamara was shoving something into the closet. She slammed the door and spun around to face her mother.

"I never get any privacy when you're around," Tamara shrieked. "Get out of my room!"

"When you can pay for your own place then you will have all the privacy you want." Celeste stood with her hands on her hips. "Now, what are you hiding in the closet and where were you so late? You know you're supposed to be in by midnight."

"It's the weekend mom and nobody else has a curfew." Tamara pouted and leaned against the closet door.

"Well, you do... now, what's in the closet?"

"Nothing." Tamara crossed her arms and glared through reddened eyes. Celeste didn't feel like a wrestling match and thought it best not to push the matter. She looked intently at her daughter wondering if she was drunk or stoned.

"Okay, fine. We're both tired so get to bed and we'll talk about this more in the morning. You have a curfew for a reason. You haven't been here long enough to know your way around and any city is dangerous for a young girl who is out this late at night. You're just asking for trouble. Come on Tamara, use your head!"

"Whatever mom.... Good night." Tamara slid into her powder room off her bedroom and shut the door. Celeste was tempted to open the closet but decided against it. Her overactive imagination was probably kicking in. She wasn't naïve enough to think that her daughter was an angel but they would address the alcohol and drugs issue in the morning. This was more troubling to Celeste especially with the harsh penalties Tamara could face if she was caught. Celeste would have to be more vigilant in the future. Ryan was usually the disciplinarian and Celeste always gave in and Tamara knew it. *Well that was going to change right now.*

Tamara stumbled bleary-eyed into the living area and sat at the bar stool at the counter looking into the kitchenette where her mother was scrambling eggs.

"It's about time you crawled out of bed, it's almost noon." Celeste focused on the frying pan, not ready to do battle just yet. "Why don't you pour yourself some coffee?" Tamara mumbled something incoherent and shuffled to the coffee maker. "Your father will be here tonight and then we'll be going to immigration tomorrow to get all our paperwork taken care of." Celeste scooped the eggs onto two plates and put one in front of Tamara.

"So, I'm not going to school?"

"Right... I'm still not used to Sunday being a school and workday here and Friday/Saturday being the weekend," she slid a glass of juice over. "No, you won't be. We all have to go to get blood tests and present ourselves at immigration with all our documentation. I'm not sure how long it will take but prepare yourself to spend the whole day."

"That sucks."

"I know but it's all part of the process. Remember we did the same thing when we moved to Saudi?"

"Yeah, I guess..." Tamara took a sip of coffee and poked at her eggs.

"Now about last night..." Celeste began cautiously. "I know you're making new friends and want to be part of the crowd and everything but I just don't want you out so late."

"I was just with Heidi... it's no big deal." Tamara put her head in her hands and rubbed her temples.

"It is a big deal. I've been reading some horror stories about girls being stalked and going missing and I just want you to be safe." Celeste paused and put her hand over Tamara's. "And, I know that you were drinking." Celeste held up her hand to stop Tamara's attempted protest. "I'm not stupid and your headache is a dead give away."

"All the kids do mom... what do you want me to do? Lock myself in my room and become a nun?"

"Of course not, but you do need to be aware of the laws here... if you're caught drinking in public, they'll throw you in jail."

"Oh mom. Don't be so dramatic!"

"I'm not being dramatic. Susan told me about someone's son she knows that it happened to. From now on you need to tell me exactly where you're going and check in if you go somewhere different. You can just send me a text and your friends won't even know that you're keeping your mom apprised of your whereabouts. Wherever you are and whatever time you want to come home, I will pick you up. No questions asked. Is that fair?"

"I think you're totally overreacting... this isn't Nigeria and there are no rebels lurking around every corner waiting to snatch me!"

Tamara stormed off, slamming her bedroom door. Celeste's stomach twirled up in a hard, cold knot.

## Deep Deceit

Celeste spent the afternoon preparing for Ryan's arrival. She tidied the suite, even though housekeeping had been there the day before and it was pretty sparsely furnished... not much for dust to collect on. But he liked things spotless. It came from his days in the military. He also liked her 'clean' so she had a long bath and shaved her legs, underarms and bikini line to the Brazilian outline he loved. She wanted to make him happy, wanted their marriage to work. She did love him and she knew he loved her, in his own way. This was a new start and perhaps in the less oppressive nature of Dubai, she wouldn't feel as intimidated. At least she had hoped so until her unfortunate altercation on the highway the day before. She wanted to fight the 'red' slip but realized it was probably a waste of time. She would see what Ryan thought when he got there.

It would be a whirlwind. He only had three days in which to finalize all the residency issues, secure the lease on the villa and sign the paperwork at the port where their container was waiting to be cleared and then moved into their new home. The timing was tight but Ryan assured her it was doable as long as she had done her part. She nervously went through the checklist in her head and hoped to hell she had had everything covered. If there were something missing it wouldn't be her fault. Her list had frayed edges from being taken out of her purse, unfolded and re-folded 20 times a day since she had arrived. She could see the list in her mind's eye as clearly as if she was holding it in her wet, wrinkled fingers as she soaked her aching muscles. Everything that was on it was crossed off. She hoped she hadn't forgotten to write something down.

She climbed out of the tub, toweled off and put on her bathrobe. She checked the tray on the dresser to make sure it had two glasses and the bottle of Chivas she had bought to welcome her husband home. Fortunately she had grabbed it coming through Duty Free since she didn't have her 'alcoholics drinks license' yet. When Susan mentioned it Celeste assumed she had been joking about the name, but Susan assured her that the name of the license was actually an *'alcoholics'* drinks license and pulled the card out of her wallet and showed it to her. She speculated that the locals figured all Westerners had a drinking problem.

Celeste wondered if they would be able to take care of that in the short time Ryan was there. It wasn't on the checklist and she didn't know if Ryan even realized they needed one. She made a mental note to bring it up. She fell asleep on the bed as she was adding to her imaginary 'to do' list.

"Where are my girls?" Ryan's voice ringing through the hallway and Tamara's greeting woke Celeste out of her slumber. Her heart began to race... was it excitement or fear? She never quite knew what to expect from Ryan, as his moods could swing from stormy to seductive in a split second. She hoped for the latter as she thought about her Brazilian shave and she felt the fluttering in her lower belly.

The door burst open and Ryan's broad-shouldered physique took over the entire doorframe. Celeste's heart skipped a beat as he covered the space between them with three big strides, holding out a huge bouquet of flowers. He swept her up in one arm and swung her around kissing her soundly on the lips. He set her down and Celeste's knees wobbled under her. As long as she had known him, his presence always sent shock waves vibrating through her whole body. Life with him was an emotional rollercoaster.

"How about a drink babe?" He spied the Chivas on the dresser. "Here sweet pea, put these in some water will ya? We'll be out in a sec." He handed the flowers to Tamara who was hovering uncertainly in the doorway.

"Sure dad." Tamara took the bouquet, closing the door as she backed slowly away.

Celeste poured two double shots of the golden spirits and handed one to Ryan. "Welcome to Dubai!" They clinked glasses and both downed the shot in one go.

"Come here you sexy thing," Ryan grabbed her around the waist and lifted her like she weighed nothing and deposited her roughly on the bed.

Celeste's heart quickened. "Ryan, Tamara's just outside," she whispered breathlessly, not really wanting him to stop. It had been weeks since they had been together and she desperately needed to feel close.

"Don't worry, I'll be quiet," he growled into her ear as he deftly parted her robe and probed her familiar body with his massive hands. Celeste succumbed to his urgent stroking, feeling a little self-conscious about the extra roll that was forming around her 40-something belly and hips. She knew it wouldn't help to fight him and the extra love handles didn't seem to faze him so she chose to get lost in the sensation as he ravenously explored her smooth, scented skin, flicking his tongue as he went.

It was over almost as soon as it started as they were both yearning for the connection and climaxed intensely together, with Celeste covering Ryan's mouth to stifle his final roar of pleasure as she buried her face in his shoulder to mask her own.

After a quick shower, Celeste poured them each another glass of scotch and they walked arm in arm into the living room to join Tamara, who smirked at them knowingly.

"The flowers are beautiful Dad," Tamara had put them in a juice pitcher that she'd found in the sparsely appointed kitchenette. "This was the best I could find."

"It's perfect honey." Celeste plopped down on the ottoman. "So, Ryan, tell us what we should expect tomorrow."

"I've got it all lined up so it should go pretty smoothly." He sat on the couch next to Tamara and draped his arm around her shoulder. She nestled into him. Celeste smiled. She knew how much Tamara missed Ryan when he was away. "More importantly, I want to hear all about the place you girls have found for us to live."

Celeste felt the stress melt away from her shoulders relieved that Ryan's mood was so jovial. She relaxed as she listened to Tamara describe the new villa, getting excited at the idea of moving in and finally having their stuff surrounding them again. She decided to wait to tell Ryan the story of the altercation on the highway. She didn't want to ruin the mood.

Celeste prayed that his rare good mood was a sign that life would return to normal soon.

## *Chapter 5*

As he promised, Ryan had everything lined up for their day at immigration and all the documents were finalized and in their hands by lunch which allowed them to also get the paperwork done for the lease on the villa all on the same day. The following day they took care of getting their container released from the port so their stuff would be on a truck the day after to be delivered to their new home.

"Well, that's a relief." Ryan looked out from the patio of the beach bar at the crystal clear waters of the Arabian Gulf and took a sip of his beer. "I can't believe we got it all done... cheers!" He clinked his glass against Celeste's.

"And, now you have a day to relax before you have to go back."  Celeste swirled the thick cabernet and inhaled the aroma before taking a sip.

"Actually, I don't... didn't I tell you?" Ryan absently punched away at his phone as he scrolled through his latest messages.

"Tell me what?"

"I've got to go back tonight. My boss on this job... actually, you remember Karl, don't you? Went to school with Donald and I... Well he's back in Saudi now, working for the Ministry and is 'technically' my boss. He's a big wheel in Saudi, right. Connected to the royal family. Well, he pulled some strings to make sure we could get everything done quickly and he's sending his jet for me. They need me back on the project... don't trust anyone else... with these guys trust is a big thing. Takes a while to earn it and once you do, you don't want to piss them off. You know how it goes..."

Celeste felt the cloud settle back over her head. Nothing had changed. But now, they were living in different countries so it wouldn't just be long days waiting for him to come home, it would be weeks! The tears welled up in her eyes and she tried to fight them back. Ryan hated it when she cried.

"Now don't pull that crap Celeste," he hissed. "I don't have any choice. Don't you think if I did I would stay longer?"

"I'm sorry... I know." Celeste tried to sound convinced but doubt ground at her insides like a termite boring through the layers of wood grain in a wall. "We just miss you. This is going to be more difficult than I thought... but we'll manage." Celeste's attempt at a weak smile was met by a cold stare that made her heart wilt in her chest.

"Well, you don't have a choice, so you'd better. We both decided that living in Saudi was too suffocating for the two of you as women." Ryan waved at the waiter for the check. "And, you can take advantage of the extra alone time to work off some of that extra weight," he poked her side and winked. "Where's Tamara? I'd like to say good bye... she doesn't know I'm leaving tonight."

"She's out with her friends but try her cell." Celeste pulled her shirt lower over her hips and bit her lower lip to keep it from quivering. She knew Ryan meant for his teasing to be playful but he didn't seem to realize it was actually hurtful. "She'd be really upset if you didn't."

"We gotta get going... they're picking me up in a couple hours and we've got one more stop to make and I still have to pack. I'll call her from the suite. Drink up!"

"That's okay, I'm done." Celeste pushed her half-finished drink away, knowing she wouldn't be able to get it past the large lump lodged sideways that pushed relentlessly on the emotional trigger in her throat.

As they pulled up to Emirates Towers, Ryan stated he had 'something' to pick up and left Celeste waiting in the car with the engine running. The 'other Ryan' had completely taken over... officious, harsh and dismissive. Actually, Celeste had counted about four different personalities her husband had displayed over the years but this one was her least favorite. She definitely preferred the sultry, seductive lover one. This Ryan always scared her, as he seemed so on edge and ready to snap at any moment. He had never raised his hand to her or Tamara but moments like these made Celeste cower inside and wonder what might trigger a violent response. She didn't want to find out.

She could tell his mind was already back on the job and, like so often throughout the years they had been together, Celeste felt like an annoyance. They returned to the suite in a flurry of expletives, door slamming and suitcase tossing. Celeste quietly sat in the corner of the couch and tried to stay out of the way.

"My ride's here already so I'll have to call Tamara from the car." He stooped down and brushed a distracted kiss across her cheek. "Good luck with the move... the realtor said she'd drop the keys off to you tomorrow and the movers will deliver the stuff the day after so make sure you're there... and, tell them in the office that we won't need to stay here another month."

She nodded silently and watched as he shrugged his broad shoulders into his cashmere sport coat. She wondered how he didn't break a sweat, even in this heat.

"I'll try to call you when I land in Riyadh." He grabbed his computer bag at the entryway and zipped it closed and wrenched the door open. "Don't worry if you don't hear from me. I'm sure I'll have to hit the ground running so I'll be in touch when..." His last words were cut off as the door shut behind him.

The tears welled up in Celeste's eyes and she let the sob she had been holding back for hours escape through her lips. She ran into the bedroom and grabbed the half bottle of scotch sitting on the dresser, poured a drink and downed it. She refilled the glass and carried both back into the living room and dropped back onto the couch, feeling the burn of the alcohol tracing the twisting curves of her intestines. It was better than the twinge of fear that threatened to envelop her. She didn't know where it was coming from but her whole being seemed to be tingling with a foreboding she couldn't quite put her finger on.

The past two days with Ryan had been both emotionally exhilarating and exhausting all at the same time. The weight of 19 years of walking on eggshells, constant negotiation, living on the edge of fear and half-truths came crashing down on her. The heaviness of the emotional burden left her body feeling battered and bruised and Celeste took another drink willing the demons to go away.

Celeste flinched as a series of church bells began chiming. *Shit, what's that... there's no church anywhere near here! Oh God, it's Tamara.* The thought sobered her slightly as she reached for her phone.

"Hello?"

"Mom? I just had a missed call from dad and now the number won't go through. Is everything okay?"

*Deep Deceit*

The sound of muffled music thumping in the background came through the phone. "Yes, everything's fine honey. Where are you?"

"Just at a friends house... what did dad want?"

"Oh sweetie, he was calling to say good bye. He had to go back early. I know he really wanted to talk to you before he left so keep trying, okay?"

"Okay, I'll try him back. That really sucks. I thought he'd be here another couple of days. I have a paper on Islam due this week and I wanted his perspective on working in an Arab country. Shit. Maybe we can Skype."

Celeste looked at her watch. "Tamara, after you talk to him I think you should come home. It's late. I can't pick you up because I've had a few drinks but call a taxi and I'll pay for it when you get here, okay? You've got school tomorrow."

"Don't worry mom... I can get a ride from someone here... bye!"

The line went dead before Celeste could ask any more questions. All parental control was slipping through her fingers. After living in Saudi for the last few years and before that Lagos, Nigeria, she knew that Tamara was simply enjoying the freedom of going out without being accompanied and not having to cover any exposed flesh from neck to ankle, as women must do in Saudi Arabia. Celeste could appreciate that but couldn't squelch the feeling of dread building in her gut. They were still living in an Arab country. Tamara might be approaching adulthood

51

chronologically but emotionally, she was still a child... had been coddled since she was a baby, mostly because of where they had lived. Living in Lagos, for safety reasons, Celeste and Tamara rarely went out without either Ryan or a driver who doubled as a security guard and in Saudi, their movements were limited because they were women and couldn't drive. Celeste wasn't sure how well Tamara would handle all this newfound freedom. She nervously checked her watch again and hoped her daughter would use some common sense.

Celeste knew there was no way she'd be able to sleep until Tamara was home safe and sound. Switching on the TV she started flipping through channels hoping to find a movie to distract her. A re-run of an old episode of Law & Order caught her attention. As she turned up the volume she realized it was dubbed in Arabic so she continued absentmindedly surfing, stealing glances at the clock on the wall every two-minutes. She gave up after the third round through the channels and picked up The National newspaper from the day before that Ryan had brought. A front-page article reported on a company recruiting women to come to Dubai as maids and then forcing them into prostitution. Another one told about a drug-smuggling ring that had been busted. Celeste put the paper down not wanting to read any further. *What was happening to this world? Everywhere you look is murder and mayhem!*

She checked the clock again and dialed Tamara's phone. It went straight to her voice mail. "Hi darling," Celeste tried to make her voice light. "Just wondering when I can expect you home. Please give me a call and let me know."

Minutes turned to hours and by 3:30 am Celeste still hadn't heard back from Tamara. Panic rose like bile in her throat. She dialed Ryan's number not caring what time it was. He should be in Riyadh by now. His phone went to a recording in Arabic. Celeste hung up. She tried Tamara's number again and got her voice mail. She threw the phone down and chewed on her lower lip and paced the length of the living room and back.

She did have Heidi's mom's number, had insisted on having it when Tamara went to spend the night. Had Tamara said she was with Heidi? Celeste couldn't remember and didn't want to worry Heidi's mom but didn't know what else to do. Should she call the police? That wouldn't end well. She would be seen as a parent who couldn't control her kid and Tamara would be labeled a delinquent. She was probably out drinking, which was illegal and she could be thrown in jail. As the scenarios whirled around in Celeste's head she started to feel dizzy and almost passed out. She sat down realizing she hadn't had anything to eat since lunch. She grabbed a banana from the bowl of fruit on the dining room table and choked it down. She shook her head trying to clear the haze and wiped a tear from her cheek with the back of her hand. She looked around at the stark, clinical decor that surrounded her. It had the bare necessities for short-term living. The temporary feel of it mocked her, made her feel displaced with no one to turn to.

She put her head in her hands and let the sobs rack her body as her stomach did a flip-flop and tried to reject the small bit of sustenance she had forced into it. She took a few deep, shuttering breaths and managed to keep it down. *Right! Enough of this!* Celeste's jaw set in determination as she reached for her purse and dug through to the bottom, searching for the slip of paper she had written Heidi's home number on. She should have just put it right into her phone. Her fingers closed triumphantly around the crumpled treasure and she clutched at it like it was a nugget of gold. She reached for her phone and shakily dialed the number, praying that Tamara had decided to stay over at Heidi's and for some reason just didn't call.

"Hullooo?" questioned a sleepy, puzzled voice at the other end.

*Oh Shit... what's Heidi's mom's name?* Celeste had a moment of panic.

"Who is this?" The voice came a little louder and this time it was more demanding than quizzical.

"Ah, I'm sorry... this is Celeste Parker... Tamara's mom."

"Oh yes, hello." Heidi's mom paused.

"I'm so sorry to be calling this late but..." Celeste's voice stuck in her throat and she swallowed hard. "Is Tamara at your house? Is she

*Deep Deceit*

with Heidi? She hasn't come home and they were together earlier so I thought she might be there."

"Jeez, I don't think so. Heidi came home just after midnight and I'm sure she was alone. We were in bed but I think she would have come in and told us."

"Can you please check? I'm really worried."

"Sure... hang on and I'll take a look."

"Thanks..." Midway through about the tenth length of pacing Celeste felt a sharp jab on the bottom of her bare foot. "Jesus!" Hopping back to the couch she peered at the metallic object protruding from her heel and yanked it out. *Shit!* She looked at the bent and crushed piece of metal that she recognized as one of Tamara's favorite earrings. Celeste put it on the coffee table and promised herself that she would fix it before Tamara saw it in the crushed mess it was... that would be after she gave her daughter a talking to about leaving her stuff lying around. She was so irresponsible...

"Celeste?"

"Mmm, hmmm, I'm here. Is she there?"

"I'm so sorry, she's not. Heidi said they were together earlier and that Tamara went to make a phone call at about 11 o'clock and never came back. She assumed Tamara went home."

"No, she didn't. Okay, I'm sorry I woke you up."

"Really, it's no problem. I would have done the same thing... I'm sure she's fine and'll be home any minute. Call me if you need anything, okay?"

55

"Sure... you know I don't even know your name," Celeste admitted, more than a little embarrassed.

"It's Karen."

"Well, thanks Karen. Sorry again for waking you."

"Don't worry about it. We'll let you know if Heidi hears from Tamara, okay? Bye now."

"Okay, that would be great, thanks." Celeste hung up the phone and her hands started shaking. She looked at the clock. It was four in the morning now... *Where the hell is she?*

Celeste's heart pounded against her chest and her breathing became labored as she remembered one other time she felt like this. The *only* other time she had been petrified out of her mind that her daughter was lost or hurt somewhere and she wasn't there to help. It was one of the rare occasions she had taken her eyes off her child when they were living in Lagos. Tamara was about three and was playing in the back yard. Celeste never left her unattended but one day ran into the house, for just a minute, to grab a glass of water. The sun beat down like a wave of invisible flames and they were both sweating buckets. She didn't want Tamara to de-hydrate... and, it was only for a second. When she got back Tamara was no-where to be seen. Celeste called out to her, thinking she was playing hide-and-seek... her favorite game. She tiptoed over to a bush ready to holler, 'gotcha'! expecting to hear Tamara's giggle burst out from behind. Celeste combed the entire area twice before noticing the gate slightly ajar.

Tamara must have reached up and unhooked the latch. Celeste hadn't realized that she was tall enough already. She frantically ran out onto the laneway just in time to see Tamara in her pink sundress with the white daisy fringe, disappear around the corner onto the next muddy, street, barren of any sidewalks. Celeste had screamed Tamara's name and went running. Thankfully she had caught up with her toddler before she had walked in front of a car or before anyone snatched her. Tamara had been following one of the many scruffy, feral cats that roamed the neighborhood. Celeste had swatted her bottom, scooped her up and run back to the house, shaking and yelling at Tamara to never, ever, go out without mommy. The thought of what could have happened had stayed with Celeste like a phantom lurking in her subconscious until this day. Now the specter was out in the open again, swooping around her, playing with her nerves with his icy cold fingers.

The recollection sent chills vibrating down her spine and back up into her scalp as she dialed Ryan's number again. No answer. "For Christ sake Ryan where are you?" She yelled at the phone, gripping it so hard the edges dug into the flesh of her palm. She started pacing, clutching her mobile and looked down at the screen and scrolled through her contact list, very few of them were in Dubai. She punched the square next to the only other person she knew and listened to Susan's phone ring.

"Hello?" A surprised but chipper voice answered on the other end.

"Hi Susan? It's Celeste. I'm so sorry to wake you."

"Actually, I'm up because I wanted to see Mitch off... he's got a pick up in about 15 minutes and he's off to the Maldives. What are you doing up so early?"

"I haven't gone to bed... Tamara didn't come home last night!"

"Holy Shit! Is Ryan out looking for her? Have you called her friends? Have you tried her phone?" Susan fired off a barrage of questions. "Honey, it's Celeste... her daughter's missing." Celeste could hear Susan call to her husband.

"That's why I called you... I didn't know what else to do. Ryan left last night, had to go back earlier than he expected and now I can't reach him. I've tried Tamara's phone and she's not answering. Susan, I'm freaking out!"

"Look Celeste, I'm sure she's fine and just spent the night at a friend's or something. Did you guys have a fight?"

"I don't remember anything in particular." Celeste's mind was racing. "We're always fighting these days."

"Teenagers! Right? But, what do I know. Look. Sit tight and as soon as I get Mitch off to work I'll come right over."

"Thanks Susan, I really appreciate it."

"No worries. I'll be over in about half an hour. Hang in there." Susan rang off.

"Sounds like your new friend has always got some sort of drama going on," Mitch shrugged his shoulders into his uniform jacket and reached for the handle of his suitcase.

"Doesn't it though? But, you've got to cut her some slack... we know what it's like to try to get settled here and we don't have a teenager in tow!" Susan handed him his hat. "You look so handsome!" She stood on her tiptoes to give him a kiss. "I sure feel for her and if I can help, why not?"

"Of course." He accepted her offer of his hat and the kiss. "You're the 'fixer' and you haven't had a project in a long time. I guess you're about due."

"Mitch, don't make fun of other people's misfortunes... or of me!" Susan swatted the air as Mitch dodged her hand. He walked to the front window and looked out.

"Looks like my ride's here." He strode towards the door and pulled it open. "Now, don't get into any trouble while I'm gone. I hope Tamara turns up soon." He called over his shoulder as the driver put his case in the trunk.

"I'm sure she will. Have a good trip and see you in a couple of days!"

Mitch waved out the car window as it pulled away from the curb.

Susan jumped into the shower and did a quick rinse, toweled off and threw on the shorts and t-shirt that she had draped over a chair the night before. She knew Celeste must be going crazy so didn't want to waste any time. Even though she wasn't a mother, Susan could imagine the angst and worry that must come along with the territory. She swung herself into her Jeep and headed towards the highway and south to Celeste's temporary accommodation in dusty *Al Barsha*. Susan knew that Celeste and her family would be so much happier in the villa in The Springs, a sprawling expat community with lots of playgrounds and manmade lakes. She wondered how much the city paid to keep the green spaces green plunked in the middle of the desert as they were. She remembered that unsettled feeling of being in limbo and thought things would smooth out for Celeste and her family once the move was done. And, it would be a much closer drive as well.

Susan had a feeling they were going to be fast friends. Like Mitch teased, she had always been attracted to people 'in need'. In all her years of psychiatric nursing and teaching she had more questions build up than were answered around the subject of the human psyche. She never tired of delving into the nuances of a person's personality and motivations, particularly those who were wired a little bit differently and didn't tend to adhere to what society told them was 'normal' behavior.

The sun was just coming up over the horizon and hit the windshield right under the sunshade practically blinding her so she almost missed her turn. Susan reached for her sunglasses. Fortunately, she caught sight of the top of the ski hill, one of the many 'over-the-top' attractions in Dubai that drew crowds to the Mall of the Emirates. This was the landmark she often watched for as her cue to exit for the mall or anything else in *Al Barsha*.

There was so much more to Celeste than someone who needed her help... Susan's intuition and years as a mental health nurse were picking up some strong signals. She sensed an underlying current of turmoil or maybe more to the point, a mysterious side that she was eager to get to know better. She had a feeling that her new friend was a complex individual.

She pulled up to Celeste's hotel/apartment complex and was thankful that she was driving a Jeep as she swerved just in time to avoid a boulder perched right in her path. As with many areas of Dubai, it was a partially completed construction site and the parking lot wasn't much more than a dirt pit strewn with debris and rocks of various and assorted shapes and sizes. She gazed slightly northeast and saw the postcard Dubai skyline of glass and chrome skyscrapers - the completed areas of Dubai that the rest of the world saw on the news and in the movies. Most of the country was still desert and construction as far as Susan had seen since she had moved there.

She stomped the dust from her feet and removed her sunglasses as she headed for the elevators. In the time it had taken her to shower and get here, Tamara had probably already arrived home and disaster would be averted.

The split second she knocked, a red-eyed Celeste opened the door and fell into Susan's arms sobbing.

"Shh, shh, honey, it's okay." Susan guided her into the living room and onto the couch. Celeste's shoulders were shaking and Susan held her and let her cry it out. Once the sobs subsided, Susan released her and went into the kitchen, came back with a glass of water and handed it to Celeste.

"I guess it's safe to assume Tamara hasn't come home yet?" Susan asked gently, putting her hand on her distraught friend's knee.

"No." Celeste's voice squeezed out in a tiny squeak and she blew her nose.

"Any word from Ryan?"

"Yes, he finally called me back and he's furious... he said he can't do anything from where he is so I'd just have to take care of it myself and get my act together and be a real mother for once." A new round of tears spilled down her cheeks.

"Jesus, that's harsh."

"He's right though." Celeste took a deep breath. "I have had a few bouts of depression over the years and I think he's gotten tired of picking up the pieces."

"Well, don't think about that now... we'll figure it out. The first thing we should do is go to the police station."

"I'm so glad you're here..."

"Sure... I'll just have to blow off Pilates but it's no biggie," Susan joked but Celeste looked like she was about to dissolve again so she quickly added, "Right then, go take a shower and change into some fresh clothes and we'll get a move on. I'll make a pot of coffee and we can take it to go!"

She shooed Celeste into the bedroom. "While you get ready, I'll do a search on my phone for the closest police station and download a map."

## *Chapter 6*

The two women sat closely together on a bench in the front foyer of the police station, not sure if they got the urgency of their message across, as the cold glare of the woman at the reception desk didn't indicate any acknowledgement. Susan knew she was Emirati. There were no foreigners working there and the woman was wearing an *abaya*, the black cloak traditionally worn by Muslim woman in the UAE and Saudi, along with a head covering or *shayla*. A couple of attempts to further their request were met with a steely stare and a clipped order to, "Wait!" accompanied by a dismissive wave of a black-cloaked arm. For the third time in an hour, Susan returned to her perch beside Celeste who fumed as she angrily punched at her phone.

"Maybe it's not working... maybe I missed a call!" She was grasping at straws. Susan started to approach the receptionist again when a door next to the desk opened and a uniformed officer approached them.

"Can I help you with something?"

"Yes... it's my daughter... she's missing."

"Ah... come." He turned on his heel and marched back through the door. Susan and Celeste obediently followed behind him down a corridor. Curious stares emanated from the cubicles that lined the way.

"Wait," again was the order, as he pointed to two chairs outside an office door. It was like they had been summoned to see the principal. They could hear voices inside.

"I've been meaning to take a few Arabic lessons," Susan said ruefully. "It sure would help in situations like this, wouldn't it?"

"What's taking so long?" Celeste stood up as the officer came out.

"This way." He motioned for them to follow him and he directed them into a conference room, waved for them to sit and turned to leave.

"Wait... please!" Celeste called as he went to close the door. "I'd like to file a missing person's report."

"One moment." He held up his hand, then turned and left.

Celeste dropped into a chair and slammed her fist on the table. "What is going on here... why won't they listen?"

"Calm down. It won't help to get all out of sorts." Susan stood behind Celeste and rubbed her shoulders. "Take a deep breath, that's it."

The door opened again and a different officer came in, followed closely behind by the woman from the reception desk. He pulled out a chair, sat down and placed a file folder on the table and the form with their contact information they had filled out when they first arrived. He ran a hand across the dark stubble on his cheek and absently scratched under his chin. It was at least a three-day growth of beard and Celeste thought he resembled a criminal more than a law enforcement agent. He looked up and stared at her through deep, coffee-bean eyes.

"You have unpaid ticket for dangerous driving," he began as he opened the file folder. "You pay now?"

"What do you mean?" Celeste was flabbergasted.

Susan gripped her hand under the table. "Officer we're here because Mrs. Parker's daughter is missing. I'm sure she'll pay her ticket today but, as you can certainly understand, she's very worried about her daughter right now."

"Why she missing?" He sat back and crossed his arms over his chest, rolling his eyes toward the ceiling, shaking his head.

"Well, she went out with some friends yesterday and hasn't returned home. The last time they saw her was at about 11 p.m." Celeste felt a little on the defensive.

"Where is your husband? He must file report."

"You don't understand. My husband is away. He's working on a project in Saudi Arabia. I have to make the report. I want to file it now... please!"

"How old is your daughter?" He shuffled through the paperwork and pushed it away with a click of his tongue, seemingly not finding what he was searching for.

"She's 18."

He clicked his tongue at her again. "She is an adult." It was a proclamation. "Not 24 hours yet, no report to file. For child, yes... adult, not until 24 hours missing."

"You don't understand. Something terrible has happened. I just know it," Celeste pleaded. "She always calls to check in." Celeste slumped in her chair.

"Are you sure there's nothing we can do?" Susan implored, looking at the woman, hoping to see a spark of maternal sympathy. The woman looked up from her notepad and shook her head and tucked a loose strand of black hair under her headscarf.

"Not until 24 hours. Now, you go." The officer gathered his paperwork and stood up. He opened the door and turned to them, waiting for them to leave. "Try hospitals."

He disappeared down the hallway and into his hidden lair. The woman, who hadn't said a word the whole time they were in the room, herded them in the opposite direction, into the waiting area and the 'cashier'. "You pay ticket here." She nudged Celeste towards the counter.

Celeste turned on her but Susan grabbed her arm and hissed in her ear, "Don't argue... you'll only make it worse. This is their world and we have to play by their rules. Just pay the ticket and then we'll go and check with Tamara's friends again." Susan gently guided her up to the counter. "We should really do what he suggested as well... check the hospitals and come back later."

Susan knew she would have to keep Celeste busy or she could be headed for a nervous breakdown. Sometimes a person who is prone to depression could snap and become catatonic when the pressure of a difficult situation got too much for them to handle. Susan didn't know how severe Celeste's condition was and didn't want to test it. She wondered if Celeste took any medication. If she did, Susan hoped she had extra with her. She knew it was difficult to get certain anti-depressants in the UAE.

After paying the exorbitant ticket, they left the police station a little more than dejected.

"Oh my God!" Celeste's hand flew to her mouth. "Susan, that's the guy who ran us off the road the other day." She pointed across the parking lot.

"Honey, how can you be sure? Did you get a good look? There are a hundred guys walking around here dressed in white. It's probably your imagination."

"Maybe you're right... but he looked right at me and I'm sure I saw him smirk."

"What a jerk!" Susan opened Celeste's door and slammed it behind her and gave it an extra hip check to make sure. "Well, we've got more important things to take care of... first, let's go and talk to some of Tamara's friends."

Susan felt her adrenalin pumping. She started going through checklists in her head, formulating questions to ask. Her love of any drama series on TV that included searching for clues or any type of medical examiner angle fed her quizzical nature. She was also a voracious reader and devoured any mysteries or suspense thrillers she could get her hands on from old time favorites like Agatha Christie to more contemporary greats like PD James, Sue Grafton and Laurence Saunders. She also combed Amazon for any gems among the self-published newbies that introduced their novels as eBooks. That was how she found her new favorite, CJ Lyons, an emergency room surgeon turned mystery writer.

Celeste called Heidi's mom again and asked if they could come by. The ride to Tamara's friend's house was painfully quiet. Susan didn't want to share some of the darker thoughts that had crept into her head to suggest what had happened to Tamara. She struggled to think of something to say to make her friend feel better. Everything that came to mind sounded too trite or preachy. So, she let the silence stretch longer.

When they finally arrived at Heidi's she couldn't give them any more information than they already had except she did eventually admit they had been at a dance club. It was a good start. Susan could feel her amateur detective alter-ego spooling up as they drove back to the hotel.

"Does Tamara have a laptop?"

"Yes, why?"

"Is it at the hotel or did she have it with her?"

"No, I'm sure it's in her room. What are you thinking?

"I'm going to drop you off at home and then go to the club and ask around to see if I can find out anything that might help. You don't have a picture of Tamara in your wallet, do you?"

"I'm sure I do... let me check." Celeste fished her wallet out of her purse. "Oh yes, here's one and it's fairly recent," She handed a photo of Tamara taken on the observation deck of the Burj Khalifa with the whole city stretching out below. "This was taken when we were here last year trying to decide if we liked it enough to move here while Ryan continued his work in Saudi. He'd had several marriage proposals for Tamara from some of his Saudi clients. We were never sure if they were serious or not. She's not even Muslim... but we decided it was time to go." Celeste's voice drifted off as she gazed at Tamara's photo. "I'm going to come to the club with you."

"No, I really think it's better if we split up. Than we can cover more ground. You get into her computer and see if there are any contacts in her address book we can call. Check emails too. There might be something there. And, you should be home just in case she calls or shows up."

"I guess that makes sense. I'm sure I have her password written down somewhere... I hope I can find it." Celeste reached over to Susan and hugged her tightly. "I don't know what I would do if you weren't here. I'm so grateful I found you." Celeste released Susan, jumped out of the Jeep and waved. Susan knew she would feel better being productive instead of sitting around waiting for something to happen.

Susan pulled up to *Allura*, the dance club Tamara had been at the night before with her friends. She briefly admired the gaping, mirror-framed entrance, took a deep breath and walked up the ruby-red carpeted stairs.

It was definitely the latest 'see and be seen' spot in Dubai. Susan and Mitch had gone opening night. One of the promoters had been on one of Mitch's LA flights and gave all the crew members free tickets. Said he loved their 'exotic' looks. Mitch flew with some of the most beautiful, poised women in the world... hand-picked by Emirates from an international labor pool. She often felt a twinge of jealousy as he headed off to work... he was so gorgeous in (and out) of his uniform she realized the ladies would definitely be circling! But, she trusted him to the deepest marrow of her bones and believed he was faithful.

The club was three floors of sparkle and bling and oozed beautiful people who pulled up to the valet in Ferraris and Lamborghinis. On opening night they had a flying trapeze on one of the dance floors, contortionists flanking the doorways and dancers swinging from stripper poles. She had since heard that the Russian mafia had established a thriving 'escort' business in the club. She couldn't help but wonder how a bunch of teenagers were able to get in.

It was the middle of the afternoon so the place was deserted other than a couple of bartenders busily stacking glasses in what looked like the start of a champagne fountain. Susan was surprised to see the ropes and pulleys and safety net of the trapeze still front and center in the cavernous main room.

"Is there a special event happening tonight?" Susan asked the bartender motioning towards the circus paraphernalia.

"No… that's permanent." The bartender's thick accent gave away his Aussie roots. "It's *Allura's* signature. We even let some of our best customers try it out… for a price, of course." He put the glass down and held out his hand. "I'm Alan, the manager… sorry it's a little dead right now. Come back at around 11 tonight and it'll be hopping. But, you might as well have a drink while you're here… what can I get you?"

"Oh, I don't need a drink, but thank you anyway. I'm wondering if you might be able to help me."

"I will if I can." He winked and leaned on the bar.

"Well, a friend of mine was here last night." Susan pulled out Tamara's photo and handed it to him.

"It was a pretty busy night... we were full to capacity and I was mostly upstairs in the VIP room... even had a surprise visit from the Beckhams." He raised his eyebrows at her, in a 'you know who I mean?' motion. "As you can imagine, we have to keep our high profile guests away from the prying eyes of the wannabes and paparazzi."

Susan was unimpressed. "I see... so, do you recognize my friend?"

The manager turned his attention back to the photo. "No, sorry. I tell you, the place is full of girls like this anyways... young, fresh, eager... you know."

"Mmm, no I don't... maybe one of the other bartenders or bouncers saw her. Maybe a waitress?"

He motioned for the bartender who was putting the last glass at the top of the pyramid and held up the photo. "Recognize her Pong?"

"No... sorry." The Filipino barman shook his head.

"The rest of the staff doesn't come in for a couple hours yet. They work late you know."

"Sure, I understand. Her mother and I are just really worried about her because she didn't come home last night. She's only 18 but she looks much older." Susan hoped she would startle him into realization that he was letting underage kids drink in his bar.

He didn't even flinch. "Sorry I couldn't be much help."

"Well, can I leave this photo with you and my number?" Susan wrote on a napkin and handed it to him. "It would be really great if you could show the rest of your staff and call me if anyone saw her."

"Sure... no worries."

"Okay, thanks."

# *Chapter 7*

Tamara opened her eyes and blinked hard to clear the blurry images floating around her like the shadows of zombies coming out of the mist. She closed them again and her hand floated up, almost disembodied, to her throbbing temple. This was worse than a hangover... and she hadn't even drunk very much. Not that she could remember anyways. ... *Jeez, what was in that last drink?* She pulled the covers up over her head not wanting to face the day yet. She couldn't remember how she got home and vaguely remembered an Arab gentleman approaching her in the club and said he recognized her from when she lived in Saudi and knew her father. Everything after that was a blur.

The sweet smell of lavender wafted from the sheets and poked at her subconscious. That was odd. Her mother never used lavender-scented anything because it reminded her of when her first husband had proposed to her in a garden in South Africa.

Tamara slowly lowered the sheets and peeked out. These weren't her sheets and this wasn't her room... it wasn't Heidi's either. She looked around the massive chamber and nothing looked familiar. Neither the dark, heavy teak armoire nor the gaudy red and gold silk rugs strewn on the floor and hanging on the walls. Who did she come home with? There had been the four of them... she and Heidi, Derek and Steve, guys they knew from school. She had never been to either of the guy's houses so it was probably one of theirs.

She looked down and saw she was wearing beautiful, powder blue silk pajamas. *Oh man! Where did I get these?* She hoped she hadn't done anything stupid.

Thankfully, her scan of the room took in an en-suite bathroom. She wasn't quite ready to emerge from her cocoon and discover whose disapproving parents she would have to face. She grabbed a bottle of water someone had been considerate enough to leave on the night table and walked into the bathroom. It took her breath away. It was stocked to the gills with salon quality shampoos and conditioners, a full-sized Jacuzzi tub and a couple of thick, plush white towels with some type of crest that seemed familiar to her, stitched in gold-colored thread. She wondered what Steve... or Derek's dad did.

As she splashed cold water on her face she puzzled over the lack of windows in the room but chalked it up to another one of the many weird architectural characteristics of some of the monstrosities she had seen that posed as homes in the Middle East. She ripped open the cellophane packaging that enclosed a brand new brush and ran it through her hair. Surely someone with this kind of money wouldn't mind... it was put out for guests anyway, right? She spied a bottle of aspirin and downed a couple with a gulp of water and re-entered the bedroom.

Tamara's eyes roamed around the room again, this time looking for her clothes. She was trying to focus but her head ached so bad every hair follicle was throbbing. There was no sign of her dress, or her purse. She had no idea what time it was since she didn't see a clock anywhere amongst the variety of knic knacs, figurines and assorted pieces of 'art'... and her phone seemed to be among the missing as well.

She would have to make herself known to the rest of the household and face the music! The situation would have been funny if only her head didn't hurt so much. Bravely, she strode across the room, reached for the doorknob and turned. The door was locked. She shook the knob and pulled again. Nothing. How strange.

"Hello?" Tamara called tentatively and waited a few seconds while rubbing her head. It had reached a new pounding crescendo. "Hello?" she tried a bit louder and banged on the door. She could feel the start of a nervous quiver squirreling around in the pit of her stomach.

# *Chapter 8*

"Well, I'm not sure anything here can help us." Celeste released a loud, defeated sigh that emanated right from her toes. "Maybe it needs a fresh set of eyes." She slid Tamara's computer across the dining table to Susan in exasperation. "I can't believe that manager wasn't more of a help." Celeste chewed on a loose piece of skin on her bottom lip... they were so dry, like the flaky skin on her legs. She still hadn't gotten used to the desert air sucking all the moisture from her body. She dug in her purse for some lip-gloss. "At least she hasn't shown up in any of the hospital emergency rooms... there's one small blessing." Celeste laid her head on her arm. She was drained and all cried out.

"Hmmm, that's true." Susan continued clicking around in Tamara's email inbox. "You know, that manager, he kind of gave me the creeps when he was describing the 'young' girls that go there. He was getting at something but I didn't want to pursue it. He made it sound like they were 'working girls'..." Susan trailed off as Celeste looked up sharply. "Uh... hey! Here's an interesting email from a guy named Steve." Susan turned the computer to face Celeste before she asked about Susan's 'working girl' comment. "Looks like he was inviting her to the club. Wasn't he one of the names Heidi mentioned? Did she give you his number?"

Celeste looked at the slip of paper Heidi had given her. "Yes, he's right here. Do you think we should call him?"

"Absolutely!" Susan grabbed the number and started dialing her phone. She nodded as she heard it ringing.

"Hi, Steve?.... My name is Susan and I'm a friend of Tamara's mom."

She paused and listened.

"Well, I don't know if you're aware but Tamara's missing."

Another pause...

"She didn't come home last night. You don't happen to know where she is do you?"

"What's he saying?" Celeste jumped out of her chair to reach for the phone about to jump out of her skin as well. Susan held up her hand and turned away.

"Uh huh... That's funny. You're sure?"

Susan finished the conversation with Steve and turned back to Celeste with a puzzled look.

"What! Tell me... what did he say and why are you looking at me like that?"

"Well, it seems at about 10 o'clock, Tamara said she wasn't feeling well and went to the bathroom."

"And?"

"And... then he saw her at the bar with a drink in her hand looking like she was expecting someone." Susan scratched her forehead, stalling.

"Come on Susan... then what?"

"He said he went and sat down with Heidi and Derek and figured she would join them when she wanted to... said something about not being her keeper. He didn't see or hear from her again. Just thought she must have gone home."

"Someone must have seen her!" Celeste grabbed her purse. "Come on... it's seven now so surely the evening staff has come in. We're going back to the club." Celeste headed for the door. "I can't sit here anymore... it's making me crazy!"

"Okay, okay... it's probably a good idea. We can go to the police station from there and hopefully they'll let us file the report. It'll almost be the magic 24-hour mark by then. Bring another picture just in case that stupid manager lost the one I left with him."

"Yeah, I recognize her." The night bartender was slicing limes for the evening's set-ups. "Good looking gal... and there were a few other guys who thought so too, even some local guy in a *dishdasha*." He dipped his head and raised an eyebrow.

"How do you know that?"

"Well, they tend to stand out in this crowd and this one in particular was a pretty scary looking dude... big guy... about six-foot-three or four," he reached under the bar and grabbed a jar of maraschino cherries and poured them into a bowl. "He pointed her out and told me he wanted to buy her a drink - a cosmo if I remember correctly."

"Did you see them talking?" Celeste asked. Her hand shook as she brushed aside a stray strand of hair that poked her eye.

"Nah... it was pretty busy and there were only two of us on last night... not sure why it was so crazy. It's unusual for a weeknight." He mopped up the mixture of lime and cherry juices that had spilled over. "I turned around and he was gone but I saw your gal and called her over to get her drink."

"Did you see her after that?"

"No, but check with Greg, the door man. He's over there now and he was working last night too."

"Okay, thanks for your help." Susan took Celeste's arm as she looked like she was about to faint. "Come on girl, don't fade on me now... we're making progress."

Celeste braced herself on Susan's shoulder. "I know... but I don't think I like where it's going."

Susan didn't reply. Her jaw set in a determined clench as they approached the doorman with Tamara's photo in her outstretched hand.

"Excuse me, Greg, isn't it?" She didn't wait for his answer. "Can you tell me if you saw this young lady here last night?"

"Yeah... the boss was just showing us a picture. She's a real looker... saw her get into a limo that pulled up at around 11 with some Arab guy... had his arm around her kind of protective-like. Looked like she'd had a little too much to drink, you know?" He winked at them.

"That 'looker' is my daughter you asshole!" Celeste advanced on him with fists clenched, about to pummel the guy.

"Look lady," he gripped her by her shoulders and held her at his very long arm's length, thwarting her advance. "I'm just trying to help... telling you what I saw."

Susan ducked under his arm and stepped in between them, her petite frame only coming up to his armpit. She pushed Celeste towards the stairs and called over her shoulder, "Sure... thanks for your help!"

She walked Celeste down the steps with her arm around her waist. "Now honey... I can't keep extricating you from the midst of potential fist fights." Susan soothed. "That guy was just a little too big... even for us to take on together."

She deposited her in the car. "Here are the keys... turn on the A/C and I'll be right back."

"Where are you going?" Celeste asked with a pout.

"To check with the valet... maybe they have records of the cars that come and go... I'm sure the limos come en mass and it's probably a long shot but it's worth a try, right?"

Susan walked back up the red stairs and Greg the doorman gave her a cold stare.

"I'm sorry about my friend... she's understandably distraught about her daughter. You understand, right?"

"Sure. What else do you want?"

"Well, I wondered if I could talk to whoever worked the valet last night... maybe they can give us some more information... or even the license plate. Do you keep records of the plates?"

"I don't know how they work that, I'm kinda new here. But there's no one there right now... maybe Alan can help." Greg crossed his arms across his massive chest. "He's in the office upstairs." He looked into the distance and took on a neutral, somewhat bored, facial expression. He had finished with her.

"Thanks. Don't worry, I'll go find him myself," Susan replied flippantly, more than a little annoyed with the guy's attitude but feeling jazzed about playing detective for real. She felt like Sue Grafton's private investigator character, Kinsey Milhone... M is for Missing!

Unfortunately, Alan couldn't help much either. Susan was glad Celeste was nowhere in earshot when he suggested perhaps Tamara didn't want to be found and that she had gone with the Arab gentleman willingly. Had Celeste been there it would most certainly have been the third time in one day Susan would rescue someone from her fury. It was getting exhausting.

Their second visit to the police station was even less satisfying as they were shuttled from reception to office, then to an assortment of conference rooms and then abandoned hallways where their breathing echoed in the silence.

A bored and very young officer took the report unenthusiastically commenting that since Tamara was 18 and there was no evidence of foul play they couldn't really do anything. It took about two hours to get that message across because of the language barrier and there didn't appear to be anyone around who could speak English or was able or willing to translate.

Susan realized it was all up to her. Her excitement at playing detective dissolved into panic. What could *she* do if the police couldn't even help?

## *Chapter 9*

When they got back to the car Celeste was despondent. There wasn't anything Susan could do to cheer her up. They drove to the hotel in silence. Susan plugged in the kettle to make some tea, helped Celeste change into her nightgown and tucked her into bed. She was afraid the depression was kicking in. She found Celeste's Prozac prescription in her cosmetic bag and brought her one with a glass of water.

"Here sweetheart, take this. It'll help you get a good night's sleep." She handed her the pill. "I'm going to stay with you, okay? I'll just crash on the couch so just yell if you need anything." Celeste nodded gratefully and took the pill. She turned away, pulling the covers up to her ears and almost immediately fell into an exhausted sleep.

Susan had no intention of leaving Celeste, knowing that it could trigger a serious mental slide if she woke up and no one was there. Susan had seen it many times and she wasn't about to let it happen to her friend. Mitch wasn't due back until the next day so he wouldn't even be home to miss her.

She poured herself a cup of tea and sat down to mull over in her mind the events of the day. Had Tamara been duped into getting into the limo? Could she possibly be wrapped up in the prostitution ring operating out of *Allura*? Susan prayed she wasn't. It would destroy Celeste. Susan crossed that off the list of possibilities since they had only been in Dubai for a few weeks. Surely it wasn't enough time for Tamara to fall into a bad crowd. Her friend Heidi seemed so sweet and her mother too involved for that to happen to her. She picked up a hotel note pad from the table and started outlining ideas to look into... post a page on Facebook with Tamara's photo, check airlines, go to the club at night and try to talk to some of 'the girls', search news media for any reports of prostitution rings, talk to Tamara's other classmates, hire a real private investigator...

She fell into a troubled sleep, dreaming about dark alleyways with scary, white-robed giants beckoning; storefronts with garish red lights blinking, and made-up harlots with two-inch false eyelashes and brilliant blue eye shadow leering from chaise lounges in window displays.

Her phone ringing seeped into her 'Moulin Rouge'-like dream and she answered, not quite awake.

"Hey hon... Did I wake you up? I thought you'd be finishing up breakfast and heading for boot camp already." Mitch's chipper voice brought her out of her reverie.

"Oh, sorry... no I spent the night with Celeste... I didn't want to leave her."

"So, Tamara never showed up?"

"No... it was a very frustrating day and we can't seem to get any help from the police even, since she's technically an adult."

"Shit, that doesn't sound good. Look, I'm about to get on my flight so gotta run but we'll talk more when I get home... maybe I can help."

"Okay... have a good flight and I'll see you tonight." Susan blew kisses into the phone and hung up as a sleepy Celeste shuffled into the living room.

"I hope you slept well because I've got a long list of things to do. I'll fix us some breakfast. It's important to keep your strength up you know." Susan tried to sound stern but the deep lines etched on Celeste's face broke her heart. She looked like death.

"I'm not really hungry..." her voice cracked as she held up Tamara's backpack. "I remembered Tamara stuffing something in her closet the other night when she came home and smelled like booze and I just went to check," a sob escaped her lips and she dropped onto the sofa.

"What's in it?" Susan asked as she took the bag, reached in and pulled out a small piece of red fabric. She un-bunched and held it up. "Wow, this is the skimpiest little dress I've ever... oh, shit..."

Celeste's moan sent a chill down Susan's spine.

"Now Celeste, don't jump to conclusions. This doesn't mean anything." She dug deeper into the bag and removed a pair of black stilettos.

Tamara sat on the bed... her hands were sore from hammering on the door. *How could it be locked from the outside? Someone's idea of a sick joke?* Tamara wasn't laughing as snippets of the night before bounced around her befuddled brain. She had a vague recollection of a limousine ride. Strange faces floated in and out of her memory like a bottle bobbing on the ocean. She lay down and put the covers back over her head and fell into a disturbed sleep.

The sound of metal rattling startled her awake and she threw the comforter off and sprinted across the room just as the door clicked closed and a key turned in the lock. "Hey...," she grabbed the doorknob and twisted it but it was too late. "Unlock this fucking door!" Tamara kicked the hard oak with her bare foot. "God dammit!" She crumbled into a heap on the floor, holding her toe in agony and started to cry. "Why are you doing this to me? Who are you?" she sputtered through the tears.

Whoever it was had brought food and left it on an ornate writing desk a few feet away. She realized she was starving but wasn't sure she'd be able to force it past the huge lump that had formed in her throat.

"What do we do now? How long do we keep her locked up like that," the young Arab raked his hand across the black stubble on his chin and sucked air through his clenched teeth.

"Patience my son," the elder gentleman cooed and leaned forward on his cushion to reach for his coffee. He inhaled the aroma and popped an almond stuffed date into his mouth. He chewed slowly and watched his son shift his weight from one sandal-clad foot to another, squirming under the scrutiny. "We have a plan and as soon as we get the money, she will be free to go."

"But what do I tell Aliya? I promised her I wouldn't take another wife and she's convinced that this girl has been brought here for me."

The old man chuckled and tugged on his steel grey beard and ran his fingers through the gold tassels dangling from his armrest. "Tell your sweet young wife that she has nothing to worry about... even though you have every right to another wife," he narrowed his eyes at his son. "Tell her she's for me."

His son winced. "Father, you already have four wives."

"What does that matter?" he growled and flung his pristine white *ghutra* back over his shoulder, then expelled a heavy a sigh. "My son," he offered in a more conciliatory tone. "It pains me to see your generation creating unnecessary turmoil in The Kingdom. Our traditions exist for a reason. A man has his needs. But, if that's too hard for you to digest, tell her she's a friend of the family. You should be able to handle that. It's not too far from the truth."

"But I don't even understand what the real truth is."

"It's not your place to question me, only to obey me. Now leave me and send in your mother. She has a houseguest to attend to and I want to make sure everything is as it should be. And... send Aliya too. She's closer to our guest's age and she seems to have a calming effect on people, including you," the old man scoffed and waved his hand at his son, dismissing him.

# *Chapter 10*

"I think I'd better call Ryan and let him know she still hasn't shown up. He'll be so angry with me when he finds out," Celeste started to tremble.

"How could he possible be angry with you?" Susan grabbed her by the shoulders to calm the shaking. "This is not your fault."

"He won't see it that way... he doesn't think I keep close enough tabs on Tamara. He went berserk one time when she was little and broke her arm falling off a swing. Threatened to k...," Celeste's hand flew to her mouth staunching the flow of the words from spilling out. She looked at Susan, panic-stricken. "Oh my God! Please don't ever tell him I told you! He's a very private person and doesn't like me airing our dirty laundry."

Susan gathered the quivering woman into her arms and gently shushed her. "Don't worry, I won't say anything. And, I'm sure he'll know you did nothing to make Tamara go missing. Now, take a deep breath and try to relax. It's just the stress of the situation that's got you all wound up." Susan knew that Celeste would have to call her husband but Celeste's reaction gave her the impression that the relationship was unstable and there was a deep-rooted fear. She had seen this reaction in abused women many times in her career and she hated the thought that her new friend was in any way being hurt by her husband.

"I can leave and give you some privacy to make your call or if you'd prefer that I stick close I can do that too... just say the word."

"Please stay. I'd feel much better if you did," Celeste's shaking had calmed down to a low vibration as she reached for the phone; dialed her husband's number and drew the handset to her ear.

"I'm really not sure what to do next," Susan pondered as she absently twirled a forkful of spaghetti. "The police were no help and we've hit a dead end with all Tamara's friends." She looked across the table at Mitch. "And, the party clothes we found in her backpack have Celeste convinced she's been drugged and forced into prostitution. I was able to calm her down and when I left she was napping but I'll have to go back in a couple of hours. She shouldn't be alone... I hope you don't mind."

"Hmmm... of course not. Maybe I can come with you and help in some way," he offered. "You know, you're doing an awful lot for this lady and you only just met."

"I know but I don't think she has any other friends and she's desperate," Susan rationalized. "And, you know I can't resist a mystery! And, she's got issues with anxiety and depression too... I see now that it's more than just the typical expat settling in stuff, so I can't walk away now. It's like being the first at the scene of an accident. With my training I'm obligated to stay until 'real' help arrives."

"I know... that's one of the things I love about you. You're such a kind person. You're in the perfect profession," Mitch started clearing the table. "Have you given any more thought to dropping resumes at the local hospitals and clinics?"

"Yeah, I'm not really ready to get back into it yet... maybe when the dust clears and Tamara's been found."

"I'm not so sure you should get too close to this, hon... what if she has gotten involved in some prostitution ring?"

"Don't be ridiculous! She's only been here a couple weeks. When would she have had a chance?"

"Okay, you're probably right. So, what did the husband say? Is he on his way here?"

"No, and I find that really odd too. I don't have kids but I think if I did have a daughter and she went missing, I would be on the first plane back, no question." Susan wiped a blotch of sauce that had fallen on her shirt.

"At first he was livid... I could hear him screaming into the phone and I was sitting across the room. Then he got all calm and quiet and Celeste said he apologized for ranting and said he was sure she'd turn up in a day or so and not to make such a mountain out of a molehill. I think he was more pissed off that she had interrupted an 'important' meeting with some high level Saudi prince! I don't think I want to meet this guy. He seems like a real asshole."

"Well, we should give him the benefit of the doubt Suze," Mitch pushed his chair back from the table. "You never know what goes on behind closed doors."

"That's true. But, I don't think they have a happy relationship and I cringe to think what does go on behind closed doors."

"Why do you say that?"

"Well, I told you she was terribly anxious and she literally started shaking at the thought of having to call him." Susan tugged on her bottom lip remembering the rest of the conversation. "She even alluded to him threatening her once but stopped when she realized what she was saying."

"Sounds like a complicated situation," Mitch shook his head.

"Yeah, it is... but I hope I can help... I want to help," Susan ran her finger around the rim of her glass. "And, honestly, you don't have to come back with me but you could do me a favor," she tilted her head and batted her eyelashes at her husband.

"Sure, what's that?"

"Didn't you say you knew an Emirati pilot whose wife works as a supervisor or as some big muckity muck in reservations?"

"Yeah, why?"

"Do you think maybe she could check the system to see if there's a record of Tamara flying the night she disappeared?"

"I'd say that's a pretty long shot. That would mean she'd been planning it in advance."

"Well, I'm trying to think of all avenues... pleeeease?" She beseeched him and clasped her hands in prayer.

"You know I can't say no when you do that," he swatted her hands. "I'll give him a call and feel him out. If the wife is high enough up the food chain, I'm sure she could check that without too much fuss. They like to show off their power so let's see."

"You're the best!" Susan planted a kiss on his cheek and grabbed her purse hanging on the back of the chair. "You do that and I'll head back to Celeste's. I'll give you a buzz later, or call me if you find anything."

"You got it. Let me know if there are any new developments on your end."

"Roger wilco!"

Susan couldn't help but feel a shiver of excitement as she ran down her driveway and hopped into her Jeep. She felt like a real gumshoe, tracking down leads and sniffing out clues. If she could just figure out what happened to Tamara... she only hoped the outcome would be a happy one.

She wanted to make one or two stops before she headed back to Celeste's. This was one mission she didn't want Celeste to come on or even know about... unless it uncovered some new information or a clue as to what had happened to Tamara.

As Susan absentmindedly navigated the early evening traffic on Sheikh Zayed Road she reviewed in her mind the places that had come up in a Google search for 'prostitution in Dubai'. She had initially typed in the search half-heartedly thinking, *Right... I'll type this and 'poof' a list will magically appear.* As it turned out, the list of news articles, video reports and Trip Advisor reviews on the very issue was endless. She narrowed it down to a few in the downtown area. Armed with Tamara's photo, she thought she would start there. If there was even a remote possibility, Susan was sure Tamara was striking enough to have left an impression if anyone in the business had seen her. It was a long shot, but the only one she could think of right now.

As she pulled up the circular driveway of the York International Hotel, the valets jockeyed for position. Susan handed her key to the closest one and took the claim ticket. She had envisioned having to scour dark alleys and seedy hotels but word on the street was that Dubai's 'ladies of the night' were found in upscale hotel lobbies and nightclubs, which Susan found oddly relieving. At least they weren't in corners of dark alleys with needles hanging out of their arms.

### Deep Deceit

She entered the lobby with her heart pounding in her throat. She was suddenly self-conscious in her yoga pants and Dallas Cowboys t-shirt. She should have planned this a little more carefully to blend in. She looked around and even if she hadn't read the headline in one of the reviews that this was a "Hotel full of prostitutes" she would have quickly drawn the conclusion herself. Her heart broke as she took a quick scan and saw about 20 young girls in tight, Lycra, micro mini-skirts and low cut sequined blouses barely covering perky breasts. They hungrily eyed the lobby door, waiting for their next meal. Each one was more beautiful than the next, yet dangerously fragile. She wondered how this blatant display of sex workers went un-noticed by the authorities. Some of the stories she had read said they turned a blind eye, which wasn't really that hard to believe from what she'd seen and heard over the past few years.

As Susan walked through the lobby, she could feel their eyes boring into her back as she passed by. Upon closer inspection, the initial impression of beauty slid away unveiling young, desperate waifs with vacant eyes.

They were from all over the world... Asia, Africa, India... it was a United Nations of call girls. Susan sat down next to a petit Asian girl. *Probably Filipina*, thought Susan. The girl had watched Susan cross the lobby with curiosity, not animosity like most of the others. Her round, deep brown eyes looked bright and inquisitive, almost playful. She was probably new to the game.

"Hello," Susan began tentatively. "My name is Susan. What's yours?"

"Suki," she said as she put a thin, red-nailed hand out. "Nice to meet you. You want to party?"

"Ah, no... thanks though... " Susan stammered as her cheeks flushed. "I'm actually looking for a friend." She pulled Tamara's photo out of her purse and held it up for Suki to see. "Have you seen her around?"

"Doesn't look familiar but I only arrive a few days ago... maybe check upstairs in the bar. The girls up there have been here longer." She smiled a sweet smile, stood up and bounced across the lobby linking arms with an older gentleman who had just entered the hotel. She guided him towards the elevators and Susan could hear her invite the man to join her for a drink. Her high-pitched voice trailed behind her getting cut off as the elevator door closed behind them.

Susan showed Tamara's photo to a few more of the girls and made a quick circuit in the bar with no luck. She hoped that Mitch was making more headway with his mission. The way things were going she wondered if they would never find out what happened to Celeste's daughter.

# Chapter 11

The tray of food sat untouched and the bathroom smelled of stale vodka and hummus. The pounding head ache and spinning room had made her stomach turn sour, rejecting all it had been forced to absorb the night before. Tamara had hung her head in the toilet and heaved the contents into the bowl with such force some had splattered out on the silk mat she knelt on. Her tears mingled with the bile that dribbled down her chin.

Once the vomiting had segued to dry heaves and finally, realizing there was nothing left to expel, Tamara's stomach stopped churning. She had waited an eternity, pacing like a caged animal, ready to spring the next time the key scraped in the lock, until she fell into an exhausted sleep.

She awoke with a start, sensing someone in the room with her. She sprung from the bed and bolted past the young girl sitting at the foot, raced for the door and grabbed the knob. It was locked. She sunk to the floor, sobbing.

"Why are you keeping me locked up in here?" she wailed and then turned menacingly towards the girl. "Who are you? Where's the key? Let me out!" she screamed.

The young girl stood up and offered an outstretched hand. "My name is Aliya," she said softly. "Please don't be frightened. You're here for your own protection." Her deep chocolate eyes watched Tamara, soft yet cautious.

"What do you mean, my own protection? Where *am* I and who the hell are you?" Tamara pushed the extended hand away and fixed her captor with a hateful glare.

"I told you, my name is Aliya. You are in Riyadh and I am going to take care of you while you are a guest in my father-in-law's house. We have been asked by your father to keep you safe."

Tamara's head started swimming again. "My father? He's here? Keep me safe... from what?"

"That's all I know. I have to go now but I will be back with your supper soon and we can talk more. Maybe play some cards?"

Tamara was too stunned to move, lulled by the calm, beguiling girl, with the long, silky black hair, who looked about her age. As she tried to process the latest news, Aliya reached over and patted her hands and then glided out of the room, her colorful kaftan swishing around her ankles as she closed the door with an echoing *thunk*.

During the years they had lived in Saudi Arabia, Tamara usually saw the local women wearing black *abayas* covering them from head to toe, seemingly floating over the ground. She dreamed of floating along with them; it looked so glamorous. But as a foreigner, she was left on the edge of their circle, never invited to join in. Here she was a 'guest' in what was obviously a very wealthy Saudi home... but she still felt more like a prisoner. *How the hell did I get to Riyadh?* She tried to gather her scattered thoughts but nothing made sense.

She had studied the Saudi culture in school when she had lived there and wanted desperately to make friends with her teenaged peers who looked so exotic and mysterious behind their veils - yearned to see what was hidden there and hear their stories. She had tried to start conversations with the local girls in the malls or salons but to no avail. So, all the friends she had made in Saudi had been other expats, her classmates at the American school.

If her father wanted her to be with this Aliya and her family, maybe she should just relax and take advantage of the inside look that she'd yearned for when she lived here... maybe they could even be friends. As she drifted off to sleep, Tamara thought she would ask if she could call her mother to let her know she was fine. Surely, her mother knew where she was.

By the time Susan had returned Celeste had worked herself into a frenzy.

"I woke up and you weren't here so I called all her friends again and no one has heard from her and don't have any idea where she went," she was walking in circles, twisting her hair round and round her right index finger. "We're never going to find her..." her words trailed off as she flung herself onto the couch. "Susan, what if something horrible has happened?"

"Come on Celeste, let's not lose focus," Susan sat in front of the computer and swirled the mouse in a circle to fire it up. "I was thinking about what our next step should be... oh, and I asked Mitch to use a connection at Emirates to see if there's any way to check passenger lists to see if Tamara got on a plane that night." Susan pulled a spiral-bound notepad out of her purse and jotted down some notes. "And, while I drove here it dawned on me that we need to contact the American embassy."

"Hmmmm..." Celeste fingered the left over pizza crust sitting on a napkin on the coffee table. "I guess it makes sense," she offered with a sigh.

"Okay, great... now hand me the phone." Susan grabbed the handset from Celeste's outstretched hand and punched in the numbers on the computer screen and handed it back once it started ringing. "Since Tamara's your daughter I think you need to be the one to talk." Susan hoped that keeping Celeste engaged would help her snap out of the funk she had fallen into. She continued writing a list of things to do so they could keep the momentum going... leaving no rock un-turned! Susan looked up from her notes as Celeste swore under her breath.

"I'm in auto-answer hell!" Celeste exclaimed as she punched yet another number on the keypad. "I think I've been through every menu offered and there's nothing that ends at a live person." She jabbed the speaker button and Susan could hear the sweet strains of on-hold music meant to transport the listener back to Arabian nights in the cool desert. Unfortunately, the intended soothing didn't appear to be working on Celeste. Susan saw her cheeks tense with every clench of her jaw.

"Just hit 'zero' and see if that works," Susan offered helpfully and walked around to sit next to her.

Celeste obediently hit '0' and the line started ringing. She sat up and smiled, a weak, hopeful smile, took it off speaker and put the receiver to her ear... and waited. Susan gave her knee a reassuring squeeze.

"A... hello?" Celeste shifted to the front of the couch and leaned forward with her elbows on her knees. "Yes, hello... I need to speak to someone about a missing person." .... "It's my daughter and I haven't seen or heard from her for two days now." .... "She's 18, why?" ..... "Yes, we filed a report with the police but they don't seem to be interested in helping find her." Celeste's voice rose. "No, we didn't have a fight... listen, she's an American citizen... can't you do something?" .... "I see," Celeste's shoulders slumped in defeat." .... "Yes, I understand... so sorry to bother you." ... "Yes, I'll call if I hear from the police.... Good bye," Celeste's voice was barely audible as she hung up. She turned to Susan and buried her face in her neck as a new round of sobs wracked her body.

"Aw honey, that didn't sound promising," Susan rubbed her friend's back gently. "What did they say?"

Celeste reached for a Kleenex and blew her nose. "They said unless there was any evidence of a crime, they really couldn't do anything and that if the police found anything to indicate something had happened to her to let them know...." She slammed the used tissue onto the coffee table with a force that made Susan jump. "God Dammit... doesn't anyone give a shit!" Celeste flung the phone across the room and it careened off the corner of the TV and clattered onto the floor. She dropped her head into her hands and a howl emanated from her very soul that pierced Susan's heart. Celeste was on the verge of a nervous breakdown and Susan knew it could go either way.

"That's it sweetie... let it all out," Susan wrapped her arm around Celeste and squeezed. "You'll feel much better... come on give me another one!" For the next hour the distraught woman alternated between sobbing and howling and sharing her worst fears and Susan 'the friend' listened with a nurse's trained ear, empathized, held the box of tissue and re-filled the water glass.

Eventually, Celeste let out a final shuddering sigh and looked at her new friend through puffy, red-rimmed eyes. "I really needed that," she smiled sheepishly. "I'm so sorry to dump on you. You must regret the day you crossed my path," she grimaced with a wry laugh.

"Don't be silly," Susan handed her another tissue. "In my line of work I've seen a lot worse than that... and for no good reason! Considering the circumstances I think you're managing really well."

Susan's phone rang in her purse. "I'd better get that, it might be Mitch with some news." She squeezed Celeste's hand and hopped up from the couch.

"Hey there... did you find anything out?"…. "Uh-huh" … "Oh?" "Okay, see you in a few then."

"What'd he say," Celeste sniffled.

"He's says he's got a lead and he didn't want to say anything over the phone so he's coming over now to tell us in person."

# Chapter 12

Ryan glared across the wide mahogany desk at the young Pakistani he had hired to manage his latest multi-million dollar construction contract. He slowly leaned forward placing his meaty forearms on desk and lacing his fingers together, gripping so tightly his knuckles turned white.

"We will bring this project in on time and on-budget... no, actually under budget," he snarled at Ali. He had hoped the educated young man would have been adept at keeping the laborers in line. Instead he'd become a mouthpiece for 'his people'.

"Mr. Ryan... sir," he began in the placating tone Ryan had come to despise. "The men have been working 16 hour shifts around the clock without a day off in several months. They're exhausted and I'm afraid someone's going to have a serious accident."

"Well, it's your job to make sure that doesn't happen," Ryan sucked in his breath through perfectly aligned, clenched teeth as the vein in his neck ramped up its beat. "And, I wouldn't have taken away their day off if you had kept the project on schedule."

"Sir... I'm not sure the men will choose to continue under these circumstances..." Ali's voice trailed off.

"Well you tell *the men* that there are 100 more where they came from for each and every one of them, waiting in line, eager to take the job," Ryan barely controlled his rage. "What you're suggesting is illegal and I will have the bastards thrown in jail or deported, and you along with them, before even one of them has a chance to raise a placard. I'd have a fresh batch here by week's end. Now, get the hell out of my office!"

He swiveled his high-backed, leather chair towards the window, waved his arm in dismissal and angrily punched a number into his Black Berry ignoring Ali's persistent pleas for at least a half day on Friday so the men could go to pray.

Ryan thought about firing his site manager right on the spot but fought to maintain control. He couldn't afford any more delays. This convention center would be the envy of the world and a huge feather in the Saudi King's *agal*. It was so close to completion, bringing in a new manager at this critical phase would be professional suicide. He was already walking a tightrope with 'the Family'. In their eyes he had lost face, but he was determined to win it back. He would find a way to spin the situation and a patsy to blame for the 'accounting discrepancies'. But it would take finesse and not just a little deceitful manipulation... but he was a pro at that.

He shook off the sour twist of dread that crept into his gut as his call went unanswered. He paced the length of his office at the top of the Kingdom Center Tower, and gazed out the wall-to-wall, floor-to-ceiling windows that overlooked the sprawling city of Riyadh. He stood at the pinnacle of his career and he wasn't going to let one misstep bring it crashing down.

Karl always answered on the first or second ring, even if only to say quickly that he was in a meeting and would call back. The incessant ringing felt ominous to Ryan. Up until a few days ago he was sure he had the man wrapped around his finger like he had so many years ago when they were attending Harvard together and Ryan had smoothed over a misunderstanding with the dean's daughter. Now, Karl was avoiding Ryan and not taking his calls.

Ryan wondered how much Karl knew. He was powerful and well respected and a relative of the Royal Family... even had the title 'Prince'. The 'House of Saud' had millions of members so his direct line to the throne was faint at best but he still carried the name Prince Khalid, which was his real name but he had adopted the nickname Karl when he moved to the US to go to university. Karl's father, the Minister of Commerce and Industry, was a second or third cousin of the King and technically Ryan's boss. Karl acted on his father's behalf as the liaison from the Ministry to all construction contractors.

## Deep Deceit

It wasn't the first project they had worked on together. Ryan sunk into the soft white leather couch in the seating area he used as his *majlis*, the name his Arab partners used for a meeting place for important discussions or political assemblies. He absently stroked and slowly spun the solid gold floor globe that was a gift from King Abdullah for a job well done. He had been the contractor in charge of building the new palace for the King's latest wife and then renovating the others to make sure they were all equally as opulent to preclude any possible jealousies. Donald would have vetoed this type of job in favor of an office building or residential compound. But, he hadn't had to cow tow to Donald's whims for years. He had taken over the company *and* Donald's wife after his untimely death in Lagos. *What a pity that was*. Ryan's lips curled as he remembered his brief courtship of his best friend's wife... another job well done as far as he was concerned. His partner's *accident* had been beautifully timed.

He sighed as his gaze took in his surroundings and he unfolded himself, stood and stretched his six-foot, five-inch frame. He wasn't born into such wealth and position like Karl; rather scraped and clawed his way to the top. Never in a million years had he thought that they would have missed the 'minuscule' amount Ryan had been skimming. When you're talking trillions, a few million was peanuts, Ryan rationalized as he walked into his private bathroom and turned on the shower. He dropped his clothes on the floor, stepped in and let the hot water beat on his tense shoulders.

His mind wandered to his family back in Dubai. He knew if Tamara hadn't shown up at home yet that Celeste would be calling again and he wasn't in the mood to deal with her hysterics. He had to get to the site and make sure the workers weren't slacking off. Tamara was a big girl and could take care of herself. She was growing up to be a much stronger and self-confident woman than her mother. She and Celeste had grown apart recently, fighting constantly and Ryan couldn't stand it. He didn't blame Tamara for not wanting to be home. She was probably at a friend's house, trying to teach her mom a lesson. Celeste just needed to loosen her grip a bit.

# Chapter 13

Susan opened the door and let Mitch in. He brushed a distracted kiss across the cheek she offered and strode into the suite towards the couch where Celeste sat, still as a statue. He gently lowered himself to sit down beside her.

"Hi Celeste," he reached out his hand. "How're you making out?"

Susan circled behind the back of the couch and sat on the arm beside Celeste and rested her hand reassuringly on her shoulder. She sensed she wasn't going to like what Mitch was about to say.

"I wish I had better news for you," he began suddenly awkward and unsure. "I know how difficult this must be..." his voice trailed off.

"Mitch... please... tell me what you've found out," Celeste looked at Mitch with round, pleading eyes.

"Well, my friend's wife works at the airport... I think Susan probably told you that," he began gently. "She has access to all the flight plans of any airplane arriving or departing from Dubai.... Along with the passenger lists."

Celeste frantically looked from Mitch to Susan and gripped his knee. "Did you find Tamara? Where is she?"

"Before I say anything, I need to tell you that my friend who gave me this information could get into a lot of trouble if anyone found out what he and his wife did," Mitch held her hand between his and took a deep breath. "You can't go to the authorities with this so I'm not sure how much it will help."

"Where is she?" Celeste jumped up and pulled her hand away and her voice rose to an ear-splitting crescendo.

Susan wrapped her arm around Celeste and could feel her vibrating like an engine overheating and ready to explode. "Sweetheart, calm down. Let's listen to what Mitch has to tell us, and then we'll figure out what to do."

Celeste's breath was coming in spurts as she tried to form her words. "Okay... Mitch, please just tell me. I don't think I can take much more of the not knowing. Anything is better than nothing."

"Okay... There was a record of Tamara's passport being used to go to Saudi."

Celeste gasped and Susan tightened her grip as she felt her friend's knees buckle.

"But they couldn't find any passenger lists that included her name," Mitch continued. "The problem is, there is also a huge number of private aircraft that come and go and, in some cases, details are omitted for security reasons. Bottom line is, we really can't tell if she actually boarded a plane or not."

"Well, the good news is Ryan is there," Susan tried to sound reassuring. "Maybe he can pull some strings to start a search from his end."

"I just don't understand," wailed Celeste. "She wouldn't go without telling me and she would need to apply for a visa... and they're almost impossible to get. You can't just waltz in and out of Saudi Arabia. Ryan would have had to make the application for her and it can take weeks!" She slumped against Susan who lowered her gently onto the couch. Celeste dropped her head into her hands and then jumped up and ran into Tamara's room. "I'm sure her passport is here," she called over her shoulder. "I saw her put it away when we got back from immigration just the other day."

Susan and Mitch followed her into Tamara's room where Celeste stood staring at the open, empty drawer to the night table. "Susan, did you open that?"

"No, I didn't... the only thing I did in here was grab Tamara's computer and brought it right out to the living room."

"Well, that's where she put her passport, and it's not there now!"

They returned to the living room and Susan went into the kitchen and poured a glass of water. She came back and held it out with one of Celeste's pills. "Here honey, take this. It'll help you calm down."

"I don't want to calm down!" Celeste screamed and hit the glass out of Susan's hand. It flew across the room and shattered against the wall. "I want my daughter!" Celeste sobbed and stormed out of the salon and slammed the bedroom door.

"Should you go after her?" Mitch asked.

"No, we'd better let her be for a little while." She walked into the kitchen and grabbed a dishtowel and started to mop up the glass shards and water.

"Careful Suz... don't cut yourself..."

"Shit!" Susan put her finger to her mouth as the droplets of bloods started oozing out. "God dammit!" She wrapped the dishtowel around her finger and frustrated tears sprung from her eyes and cascaded down her cheeks as she sat cross-legged on the floor.

Mitch shook his head. "Sweetie, you're over-tired and this thing with Tamara has you tied up in knots."

"No it doesn't," she snapped.

Mitch crossed his arms and tilted his head. "Oh, really?"

"I'm sorry... I guess I am sort of caught up in this... but," she raised her hand as he opened his mouth to speak, "I'm not going to stop now. I've got to help Celeste... I have to see this through. She doesn't have anyone else." Susan ran the tap water over her finger and held it up for closer inspection. "I think I'll live." She smiled at her husband.

"I wasn't going to even suggest that you would stop helping... I know that would fall on deaf ears," he sighed. "I just want you to take care of yourself... don't forget to eat, okay?" He kissed her on the forehead. "I've got to go back home and get some sleep. I have a midnight pick-up... a Hyderabad turn-around, and if I'm going to get at least six hours of sack time before then, I gotta go now. Are you going to stay here?"

"Yeah, I really should," Susan put her head on Mitch's shoulder. "I'll give her an hour or so and then I think she needs to call her husband. It's the most logical next step."

"You can't tell him why you believe Tamara is there... remember?"

"I know... I'll think of something."

A pitiful, mewling sound, like a kitten looking for its momma at feeding time seeped into Susan's subconscious, stirring her from a troubled sleep that had gripped her. Reaching behind her, Susan felt for the reassuring warmth of Mitch's body and felt the back of the couch. *Shit!* She had fallen asleep.

As Susan shook herself awake she realized the whimpering was coming from the bedroom. She swung her legs to the floor and pushed her fatigued body to an upright position, and was already halfway across the room purely on instinctbefore her sleepy brain could break through the haze, following the sorrowful sound that had escalated like a foghorn.

She knocked on the door while turning the knob and pushing it open. "Celeste, honey? It's me..." Susan's voice trailed off when she took in the scene in front of her. Celeste was curled up in the corner of the room, rocking back and forth, her arms wrapped around her knees, staring into space. The sporadic moans were alternately fading to a whimper and then bursting out loudly like verbal projectile vomit.

Susan recognized the symptoms and knew Celeste was having a full-blown mental health crisis... an emotional breakdown. She grabbed a sheet off the bed and wrapped it around Celeste's shoulders, crooning gently in her ear. "Come on... shhhh... it's going to be alright. I'm going to take care of you. You'll be just fine." Susan continued her soothing reassurances as she guided Celeste back to the bed, stretched her out and tucked the blanket under her chin. In the warmth of the desert climate most people set the A/C at 80 degrees Fahrenheit or so, which was comfortable. Even at that, Celeste was shaking uncontrollably but Susan knew it wasn't from being cold. Her body was reacting physically to too much emotional stimulation, which Celeste was unable to handle any longer. *The meds she was taking for anxiety wouldn't be enough to combat this latest episode,* Susan thought as she dialed 999, Dubai's emergency number, on the phone on the bedside table. She sat close, stroking Celeste's hair, pushing it away from her face. It wouldn't be prudent for her to attempt to get Celeste to the hospital on her own... even though Susan was sure her catatonic state would persist until she had proper medication she didn't want to take a chance of an emotional outburst happening on the highway between the hotel and hospital.

## *Chapter 14*

The bright, cheery borders halfway up the stark white walls held brilliant yellow sunflowers skipping in happy circles around her, mocking her from their unfair vantage point, propped up by the wallpaper glue underneath. If she had any energy, she would claw down the incongruous, weak attempt at creating a welcoming, friendly atmosphere. There was nothing friendly about her surroundings.

Celeste rolled onto her side and pulled the sheet up over her head, willing herself to be anywhere else. She winced as the needle from her IV wobbled inside her hand, pushing against the delicate walls of the vein it inhabited. She hated hospitals.

*I'm such a pathetic excuse for a mother... can't even hold it together to help my daughter.* Silent tears welled up in her eyes and spilled down her cheeks. *How long have I been here? Where is she? Why can't anyone help us? Where's Ryan? Why isn't he here?* The questions swirled in a dizzying fjord with no answers and increasing numbers of questions springing from the last. Memories of her last hospitalization came crashing down... threats

118

from Ryan to have her committed, pleading with him to take her home, promising she'd never try anything like that again. She remembered the black tar stains on the hospital sheets after her stomach had been pumped... pictured the empty bottle on her night table. *I've been doing much better. I've been trying so hard! Does he think it's my fault that Tamara's missing? Was I suffocating her? She's just got to be all right.*

"Mrs. Parker, it's time to have some lunch," the duty nurse's voice broke into her tortured reverie. "How are you feeling? Do you think you can eat something dear?" her British lilt questioned gently as she pulled the covers back from Celeste's face. She smiled warmly. "There now, let me just adjust your bed a bit." She pushed the button and the motor mechanism under the bed chugged away as the back of the bed rose, taking Celeste's limp body with it.

"I'm not very hungry," she managed to croak. Her voice sounded foreign to her ears.

"Just try a little bit of the pasta and I'll bring in some ice cream too." She rearranged the thin blanket around Celeste's knees. "The doctor will want you eating normally before he'll sign your release form."

"You're awake," Susan peeked around the curtain. "How are you feeling?"

"Like hell... how long have I been sleeping," Celeste mumbled twirling the pasta absently with her fork.

"Oh, it's got to be going on 15 hours or more," Susan pulled the chair up next to the bed as the nurse finished checking the IV and silently exited the room, like she was floating, her white shoes barely whispered against the floor.

"What happened? Last thing I remember is Mitch coming over..." her voice caught in her throat and Susan squeezed her hand. "I'm so sorry Susan... I really tried to keep it together. It's too much to handle without Ryan here," she looked desperately at Susan. "I don't understand why he's not here."

Susan handed her the glass of apple juice. "Actually, he's on his way... his flight should have landed about an hour ago and he said he would come straight here," Susan assured her. "I found his number in your phone and called to let him know you were in the hospital."

"Was he angry?" Celeste whispered.

"Angry? Why would he be angry? He's worried about you and Tamara, of course. Said he would take care of everything when he got here. Maybe with his connections and, I hate to admit it but, since he's a man, hopefully he'll be able to make some headway with the police." Susan pulled out some magazines from her oversized purse and put them on the lunch table.

Celeste shivered thinking about the 'controlling' Ryan who would more than likely descend upon them soon but managed a weak smile for Susan's benefit.

"He was sure that Tamara would 'turn up',"
Celeste thought out loud. "Maybe he's finally
realized something's not right. And I didn't do
anything wrong," Celeste went on quickly seeing
Susan's puzzled look. "Did you tell him that we
think she's in Saudi?"

"No, I was worried about you and thought
we should wait until he got here to explore that bit
of information any further."

"Right..." Celeste yawned. "I think they must
have put something in my IV." She yawned again.
"I probably should sleep a little more so..."

"Oh sure... don't you want me to stay until
Ryan gets here?"

"No, I'd rather talk to him first... alone..."

"Okay... as long as you're sure." Susan stood
up and slung her bag over her shoulder. "I really
don't mind."

"I'm sure."

"Fair enough," Susan smiled and kissed
Celeste on the forehead. "Sleep is the best thing for
you now. You've got to regain your strength... for
Tamara's sake."

"I know..." Celeste mumbled as she drifted
off.

"Where the hell's my wife?" Ryan stormed onto the
floor Susan had told him Celeste was on. "I was
told she was here." He leaned over the counter

breathing heavily on the petite nurse sitting at the nursing station.

"S-s-sorry sir... your name?" She frantically shuffled the patient submission forms in front of her.

"Ryan, Ryan Parker," he took in her name badge, *Jenny, Student Nurse*. "Jenny..." he said gripping the edge of the counter. "What room?"

"Oh, yes... Mrs. Parker. She's in room 3B..."

Ryan was already halfway down the hall and didn't hear what the young nurse said, and didn't care.

*Simpering idiot...what the hell business does she have looking after people? Incompetent bitch... this is all I need. Fuckin' Celeste. What a time to pick to have a breakdown. What a pain in the ass... never should have married the clinging, whiny woman. If she hadn't been pregnant I wouldn't have... sure felt good to stick it to Donald though... fuckin' do gooder. Where the hell is this room? Way down the end of the God Damned hallway, of course.*

# *Chapter 15*

Tamara paced the room. How long were they going to keep her locked up? What did they mean they were keeping her safe? If her father knew where she was surely he would come get her soon. What about her mother? And, why was she in danger anyway? If she was a guest, why was she locked in this room? The questions swirled around in her head making her dizzy.

There was a soft knock on the door and Aliya breezed in. "Hi Tamara, how are you today?" She smiled sweetly. "I brought a few games." She held out a large straw basket. "I thought we could spend some time together." She walked over to the sitting area and lowered herself onto the silk rug and motioned for Tamara to join her.

"Uh, I'm okay, I guess," Tamara hesitated briefly and then dropped down cross-legged across from her new friend. "Can I leave my room today... maybe have dinner with your family?" She busied herself lifting the items from the basket Aliya had brought. She didn't want to jeopardize the fragile connection she had to the outside. If she played along and didn't push, maybe Aliya would tell her more.

"I think that would be lovely," Aliya said. "Let me ask my mother-in-law and we shall see okay?" Aliya spread the games out on the rug... Monopoly, Clue, a deck of cards, Trivial Pursuit.

"You don't have any video games?" Tamara wondered out loud, and then realized there was no computer or TV in the room.

"No, my father-in-law doesn't allow them... my father didn't either. There's one computer in the house and it's in my father-in-law's office and he keeps that locked all the time." Aliya set a stack of green and yellow cards on the board and spread out the colorful play money. "Which would you like to play?" Aliya asked reaching for Monopoly. "This one is my favorite."

"That's fine," Tamara sighed. "But, I've never played it so you'll have to teach me."

"I can do that!" Aliya opened the game board. "What piece would you like to be... the shoe, the thimble, race car, top hat or iron? There used to be a little Scottie dog too, but I think my niece took it home with her the last time we played."

"The race car, I guess," Tamara reached for her piece thinking how odd it was that Aliya seemed so at ease for someone who was holding another person prisoner. That was how Tamara felt... not like a guest at all. But, she would *play the game* until she could figure out what to do. She was certainly comfortable and being well fed so didn't feel in any immediate danger. If she could get to that computer, she'd send a message to her father.

First she had to find out exactly where in Riyadh she was and who these people were.

Aliya was busily counting out each of their starting cash, happily chatting away. "We've all been invited to a wedding you know and Yousef, my husband, thinks it would be nice for you to come with us. I'm not sure if you can, but we'll see"

"I would love to see a Saudi wedding," Tamara said as her mind started sifting through how she would use the opportunity to her advantage. "When we lived here we didn't really get to see much inside Saudi life."

"Well, hopefully we can change that. And, you can ask me anything about our culture too. But later... now let's play."

"You go first... it's your game and your house," Tamara handed Aliya the dice.

## *Chapter 16*

Celeste awoke to find Ryan glaring down at her from the foot of the bed. His look sent chills coursing through her like a full body brain freeze.

"Well, you're finally awake," he said and his face softened into a half smile. "How are you feeling?" He walked slowly around to her side and took her hand.

*I'm just imagining things. He's just concerned.*

"I'm much better now that you're here," Celeste clung on to Ryan's hand and smoothed the sheets awkwardly with her other, IV-invaded one.

"I came as soon as I could," Ryan smoothed the hair from Celeste's forehead. "Some woman named Susan called me... who's she again?"

"She's my friend I met at the beach boot camp, remember I told you about her?"

"Yeah right... I'm not sure I'm comfortable with her knowing all our business," Ryan said. "She even mentioned Tamara hadn't shown up yet. Why does she know about that? Haven't you heard from her?"

"Well... I..." Celeste tried to sit up, still gripping Ryan's hand. "No, Tamara's still missing and it was so overwhelming. With the move and you not being here, it was too much to handle. I just lost it. But I'm okay now," Celeste rushed to go on. "Susan's been so kind and is helping to find Tamara..." Her voice trailed off as Ryan pulled his hand away and started pacing.

"I'm only gone for a few days and everything's already a mess," Ryan spun around with his hands on his hips. "I've got some serious issues at work and now this," Ryan swept his hand toward Celeste and let it drop to his side. "And, to top it all off I get a call from the moving company saying they're still waiting for instructions on where to deliver our furniture."

"I can't believe you're thinking about work and furniture," Celeste's ice-blue eyes widened and then hardened. "What about Tamara? What about me?" Celeste felt a rush of maternal rage. "Isn't she the most important thing right now?"

"Of course she is... don't be so melodramatic Celeste," Ryan said. "It's just that the Minister wants to see me and you know that can't be good." He continued pacing. "I'm not sure how long I can stay. So, if she hasn't turned up yet I guess I should go to the police... you did already didn't you?"

"Of course I did," Celeste laid back on her pillow. "They wouldn't listen to me because she's 18 and there's no evidence of a crime... I already told you that."

"Well, what do you suggest we do then?" The vein in Ryan's neck was pulsing.

"Actually, I think I know where she is... sort of... and we need to get the Saudi police involved," Celeste said.

"For shit's sake Celeste, what for?" Ryan asked.

"We have a good lead from someone who works for Emirates who says Tamara's passport was used the day she went missing... The system showed her going to Riyadh but there's no record of her on any commercial flight."

Ryan went pale. "Who told you that?"

"I can't say... they broke the rules helping us so we promised not to tell anyone."

"Who's we?"

"Me... and Susan and her husband," Celeste said.

"Susan's husband knows about this too?" Ryan scratched the stubble on his chin. "Jesus Celeste!"

"You weren't here and I didn't have anyone else to turn to... Susan's been a huge support for me."

"Well, now I'm here and we don't need anyone else getting involved," Ryan said. "As soon as we can get you released we'll both go back. It doesn't make sense to me but if she's in Saudi, I know people who can find her. I'll make a few calls now and get a visa lined up for you." Ryan was already dialing his phone and swore under his breath as he left the room.

# *Chapter 17*

"Kill him," the Minister waved his hand and smoothed his, spotless, starched, white robe then reached for his coffee.

"I'm not sure that's the best course of action, cousin," Mohammed stopped pacing the minister's office and glided into the chair opposite him. He gazed at the bronze falcon adorning the corner of the room with the name of the office engraved on a sash gripped in its talons – *Kingdom of Saudi Arabia, Ministry of Commerce & Industry*.

"I didn't ask your opinion... but, please, tell me, why do you think that? He's broken the law."

"Yes, he did... but perhaps we arrest him instead," Mohammed poured himself a coffee. "Let the courts decide his fate. He stole from the Royal family, which is punishable by death. It could be a public hanging to make an example for others who consider stealing from us!"

"Ah, but that would draw the world's attention," said Bashir. "I prefer to keep our affairs private, especially when it comes to dealing with our American brothers."

"But his daughter is still a guest in my home. What do we do with her?"

"Are you not taking care of her? Is she not happy?"

"Of course, Bashir, but you must realize, American woman are different from our women... they don't understand our customs, our culture," Mohammed started pacing again. "And, Fairuk said he followed her mother to the police station in Dubai. She was with another woman. What does Khalid suggest?"

"Khalid? He doesn't know and I'd prefer to keep it that way. He's much too Westernized to understand. His U.S. education serves us well when dealing with American corporations but he would not agree with our methods in this matter. And, I'm not worried about the police in Dubai... they will not find any reason to pursue an investigation and any witnesses will say she came of her own free will," Bashir fingered the signet ring on his hand, stroking the 2-carat diamond in the centre. "Make sure you keep her comfortable until we find a resolution to our problem. He must suffer," said Bashir.

"I understand," Mohammed slowly stirred the milk into his coffee. "Perhaps there's another way to make him pay."

"I'm listening."

Ryan slammed the car door and hammered his fist into the steering wheel. *Dammit all to hell!* He thought. *If Celeste had just been able to hold it together a little longer, everything would have worked out according to plan. Jesus fucking Christ!* Starting the engine, he jammed the rental into reverse and squealed out of the hospital parking lot. He headed straight for the York International where he knew the prostitutes were plentiful. He had to be 'taken care of' or he was going to explode. His Black Berry bugling 'reveille' jangled him back to the present and he snatched it with his left hand while maneuvering the steering wheel and hugging the tight curves of the roundabout as he headed for the highway.

"Yes, Parker here," Ryan growled into the phone.

"Ryan, it's Karl... where are you?"

"Had to make a quick trip to Dubai, didn't Ali tell you? I should be back in a couple of days. I've got some family business to take care of. I left everything in good shape and told Ali to call me if anything went sideways."

"You picked a really bad time Ryan, the Minister's been asking for you."

"I know... Ali told me... Fuck!" Ryan swerved to miss the red and yellow taxi that moved into his lane without signaling. He was pleased he had chosen to rent a high performance sports car rather than the 'reliable' mid-sized sedan Celeste had leased.

"There's no need for that!" Ryan could hear the contempt in Karl's voice and knew if it were up to Karl, Ryan would be fired from the project.

"No, not you... Goddamed taxi drivers... they all need to go back to Pakistan," Ryan gripped the wheel with his free hand and kept his eyes peeled for cops and cameras. He didn't need the hassle of being pulled over for talking on his phone while driving. "Do you know what it's about?"

"No, he didn't say but you'd better get back as soon as you can. As you know, he's not a patient man. Did you take the jet or are you flying commercial?"

"I flew commercial but may need you to send the jet back for us," Ryan said. "And, Karl, I may need your help fast-tracking a visa for Celeste."

"Why? I thought you were settling the family in Dubai and commuting yourself."

"Celeste's been ill and we're having trouble with our daughter... but I'll explain later. The traffic's really bad so I've got to go... " Ryan hung up before Karl could ask any more questions. Ryan knew exactly why the Minister wanted to see him but he'd be damned if he was going to tell Karl. He'd just get into the middle of it and fuck it up. Ryan would handle it himself. *Why did Karl have to move back to Saudi? Life was simpler when he was back in the States. He was just way too inquisitive.*

Out of the corner of his eye, he caught the exit sign for the World Trade Centre roundabout. "Shit!" He swerved, cutting across three lanes

132

knowing that if he missed the exit it would be 30 or more kilometers before he could double back. He ignored the horns and screeching of breaks he left in his wake. His mind was racing... the project behind schedule, Celeste's breakdown... and where the hell was Tamara? The more days that went by without her 'showing up' the more Ryan suspected he knew what might have happened to her.

"Assholes," Ryan swore as he slowed to a stop at the first set of lights on the roundabout and drummed his fingers on the dashboard.

# Chapter 18

The smell of triple-cheese, deep-dish lasagne, Mitch's favourite, wafted through the house like a floating caravan of magic carpets, laden with seasoned tomatoes and mild melted mozzarella. Susan knew she would have to put on her very best convincing act to get Mitch to agree to her plan. She looked in the mirror, puckered her lips and applied a light coat of gloss over the frosted pink lipstick. They screamed, 'Kiss me!' and she had no qualms about playing the 'sex' card, as long as it worked. He was usually tired after a trip from Los Angeles but the long haul flights always had two cockpit crews and he had told her the return flight was the other captain's leg so he would have had a fairly decent sleep. He was due back shortly and would be hungry. She would feed and pamper him and take advantage of his weakened state to pitch her proposal to go to Saudi with Celeste.

Celeste had called her from the hospital in a panic after Ryan had left. She told Susan that he was taking her back to Saudi with him. Susan reassured her everything would be okay and started hatching a plan... but first she had to convince Mitch to go along with it.

## Deep Deceit

She had changed three times already, not wanting to over do it or make him suspicious. It really wasn't a big deal. Celeste needed her and she was going. So she would have to play down the negatives and basically present it in passing conversation. She'd worry about the visa application to enter The Kingdom once she got him to sign the letter of permission, which she would need in order for her application to be considered. A letter of permission from your husband was required to do just about anything in the UAE and Saudi Arabia. She didn't know about other Middle East countries but figured it was the same no matter where you went in the region. Dubai seemed very cosmopolitan and forward thinking on the surface but she had needed the 'permission' letter to open a bank account, to get her drivers license and to have her very own alcoholics drinks license. She would also need one if she decided she wanted to work while they were in Dubai. She reached for the checklist she had already started and added: Borrow an *abaya* (or two) from Katie. She knew she would be required to wear the black cloak and headscarf to cover her from head to toe and her friend Katie had a whole collection of them as she had several clients in Saudi.

After deciding against the black slinky number and the powder blue negligee in favor of the red and purple flowered, mid-thigh sundress Mitch had brought back for her from his recent trip to the Maldives, she was ready for her husband to come home.

She slid on her American flag oven mitts, a gift from one of her friends when they left North Carolina, opened the oven and pulled out her masterpiece. She inhaled the aroma and smiled as she heard a car pull into the driveway. She trotted into the dining room and lit the candles on the table, took a quick look at herself in the mirror in the foyer and opened the front door to Mitch coming up the walkway as the Emirates driver backed out of their driveway.

"Hey hon," Mitch greeted her and kissed her cheek. "You look terrific... what's the occasion?" He continued past her into the house dragging his suitcase and flight bag behind him.

"Oh nothing... I just missed you, that's all," Susan closed the door and followed him into the bedroom.

"Something smells amazing... is that lasagna?" He loosened his tie and hung his uniform jacket in the closet.

"Yes, it is," Susan reached for his bag. "Do you want me to put this stuff in the wash?"

"That would be great... it's pretty smelly... my gym stuff is in there," Mitch walked into the bathroom. "Do I have time for a shower before we eat? I've gotta wash this airplane smell off," he said already turning the tap on.

"Sure, no problem. I'll pour us a glass of wine," Susan answered the shower curtain. "Don't be long... I'm starving"

She gently closed the bathroom door and congratulated herself for maintaining a level of 'nonchalance'. She plated the lasagna, carried it into the dining room and set the two helpings on the placemats. She opened the bottle of Cabernet and left the cork out to give it time to breathe.

"Be right there Suze," Mitch called from the bedroom.

"Take your time... it's cooling off and the wine is breathing," she called as she stole another glimpse in the mirror and added one more swoosh of gloss to her lips.

"Okay, what's up?" Mitch startled her as he came around the corner and wrapped an arm around her waist drawing her in for a hug. He nuzzled her neck. "Whatever it is, I approve. You smell amazing!"

"Mmmm, thanks," Susan said almost forgetting about her carefully laid plan. She pulled back a bit and kissed him softly, pulling away as the pressure from his lips became more urgent. "Now, now... hold on Romeo... let's eat before it gets cold."

"Aw, you're no fun," Mitch released her and smacked her bum as she walked away. "Probably just as well though. I'm sure I'd fall asleep half way through... I hope I don't do a face plant in my pasta!"

"I'm sure you're exhausted," Susan reached for his glass and poured a liberal splash of red.

"Thanks. I am tired but happy to be home." Mitch took a bite. "Oh my God, this is the best yet!"

"Yeah right. You say that every time," Susan laughed and put a forkful into her mouth. "Jeez, you speak the truth, it is amazing... if I do say so myself."

They ate in companionable silence for a few minutes.

Susan took a long swallow of her wine. "So, I think Celeste is feeling a little better," she began slowly, letting her statement sink in.

"Oh yeah, is she out of the hospital yet?"

"Not yet, but I spoke to her just before you got home and she told me they're releasing her tomorrow. Ryan finally got here so he'll take her back to the hotel and then they'll be headed to Saudi together in a few days."

"Hmmm..." Mitch seemed preoccupied savoring every mouthful so Susan took a deep breath and plunged headlong into her rehearsed speech.

"And, I think it's a good idea if I go too... you know I'm a nurse and highly qualified to care for someone with Celeste's condition and I think she needs a friend with a little more empathy to tag along and Ryan's so busy with his job and we think that Tamara's there anyways so I can help her continue the search while we're there... I know Ryan can expedite my visa, but I'll need you to give me a letter of permission, which I've already drafted so I just need your signature..." Susan's voice trailed off as she realized Mitch had stopped eating and was staring at her, his eyebrows knitted so closely together they'd turned into a uni-brow.

"Are you crazy?"

"What? Why? It's no big deal," Susan sat back and crossed her arms.

"I don't care how great this lasagna is and how hot you look tonight, you're not going to Saudi Arabia... it's ridiculous to even think about it."

"Why is it ridiculous? I just want to help a friend."

"A friend you just met, who suffers from depression and whose husband is borderline abusive."

"You don't know that." Susan twisted her napkin around her finger, realizing that she was not winning and wondering how she would bring Mitch around. "I think he's just stressed. His project is going sideways on him and he's getting a lot of pressure... you know he's working for the royal family, right? I think he'd really appreciate having me along."

"Think? You mean you haven't run this hair-brained scheme by him yet?"

"Well, no," Susan saw her chance. "I wanted to check with you first. We could talk to him together and then maybe you'll feel more comfortable."

"I don't know Suze," Mitch wiped his mouth and tossed his napkin onto his empty plate. "We haven't even met the guy yet and there are too many unknowns when traveling there. I need to think about this."

"Okay, we'll both sleep on it." *And then we can go see Celeste together in the morning and propose the idea*, she thought to herself. Susan

139

forced a smile and started clearing the table. She didn't want to push it.

The next morning as they drove to the hospital Susan tried not to grin too wide. She had worn Mitch down and he had finally agreed she should go to Saudi with Celeste, *if* he met Ryan and got a good vibe from him; *if* Susan called him every day and; *if* she was able to get a visa to go. There were a lot of ifs but Susan was determined to make it happen.

Mitch pulled into a parking spot that had just been vacated by a Maserati. "I guess this is a VIP hospital." He put the Jeep into park and put his hand on Susan's knee turning to face her. "You know I have some serious reservations about this, right?"

"I know, but I swear it'll be okay," Susan squeezed his hand. "I can handle myself."

"I hope so," Mitch sighed.

They walked into the hospital and up to Celeste's room, knocked and pushed the door open. Celeste was up and dressed and sitting on the visitor's chair.

"Hi guys," she stood up and reached out to Susan. The two women embraced. Celeste held out her hand to Mitch. "Thanks for coming," she motioned for them to sit. "The doctor signed my release forms already so now I'm just waiting for

Ryan." She dropped her toothbrush in the small overnight case Susan had brought with them the night Celeste had her breakdown. She zipped it up and set it down on the bed.

"How are you feeling sweetie?" Susan gently touched Celeste's flushed cheek.

Celeste leaned into Susan's hand and smiled, "Ready to get the hell out of here!"

"I'm sure you are," Susan smiled back. "When's Ryan coming?"

"He should be here any minute... and I told him what you, I mean *we*, have in mind... I didn't want to blind-side him. He's not big on surprises."

"What does he think about Susan going with you?" Mitch asked.

"Oh, he's warming up to the idea," said Celeste. "He wasn't thrilled at first but he realizes it would make it easier for both him and me."

"How easy will it be for Susan to get a visa?"

"Mitch... let's work the details out when Ryan gets here, okay?" Susan opened the drawer next to the bed. "Did you empty all the drawers, hon? You don't want to forget anything."

"Yes, I think so... doesn't hurt to check again, thanks."

Ryan punched the up arrow with the side of his fist for the third time and glared at the glowing green digital numbers as they slowly counted down to the lobby level. *Shit! The crap Celeste gets into her head. Why couldn't she just leave well enough alone... Jesus!* Having Susan along would be a pain in the ass. The woman was too clever... and nosey. But he'd find a way to work it to his advantage. He couldn't make a big deal of it. If he claimed that he couldn't get her a visitor's visa it wouldn't be believable. He'd never had problems before getting visas for family and friends to visit. So, he'd just play it cool, act like the loving, doting husband, have her look after Celeste for a week or two, and then send her along her merry way. If she was entertaining Celeste, he'd be able to take care of things without worrying about her or Celeste getting in the way. He'd win her over with his charm, which he could pour on anytime he wanted. It had served him well over the years.

The elevator dinged, the doors slid open and Ryan stepped aside to let a hospital bed and two wheelchairs out before sidestepping around behind them into the empty space. He furiously pressed the 'close door' button over and over as a family carrying flowers and helium balloons with the words 'It's a boy!' rushed over calling 'hold the elevator'. The voices got cut off as the doors closed with a satisfying *thunk*.

Ryan watched the numbers click by, both fists clenched at his sides. His jaw worked in rhythm with the whirring elevator cables. He took a deep breath through his nose. *Okay, game face on Parker*, he commanded himself. *We'll work this to our advantage. Someone else can deal with her histrionics and it won't cost a thing.*

He willed a smile to his face as the elevator door opened. He would exude charm and sincerity. He nodded at the nurses, fortunately a new batch that hadn't witnessed his interaction with the night duty nurse. He drew up to his full six-foot-five height.

"I'm here to pick up my wife, I understand the doctor has released her," Ryan addressed the youngest and prettiest of the three sitting at the desk going over charts.

"Oh, ah,... yes, of course," the girl stuttered and blushed. "What's your wife's name?"

"Celeste... Celeste Parker. I'm Ryan Parker. I'll just head down... I know which room it is, thanks."

"S-s-sure."

He could hear them whispering and giggling as he walked away. *Simpering idiots.* He continued his confident swagger down the hall and as he approached Celeste's room could hear the low murmuring of both a male and female voices. *Shit! The husband's here too. Slight deviation in approach but still controllable.* He strode into the room with a smile, inside he was puffed up like a cobra, watching carefully, sussing the situation out, ready to strike with his sweet venom.

"Hello sweetheart," he went first to Celeste, kissed her on the cheek and wound his left arm protectively around her.

"Hello, I'm Ryan," he held out his hand to Mitch first, establishing the pecking order in the room.

"Nice to finally meet you," Mitch smiled and grasped Ryan's hand. "I wish it was in better circumstances but maybe we can grab a beer sometime."

"Sure… and you must be Susan." He turned his megawatt smile on Susan as she took his hand. Still holding her hand, Ryan gently removed his left arm from around Celeste's shoulder and warmly encompassed Susan's hand between both of his. "I hear I have a lot to thank you for… you have no idea how worried I've been but I understand my wife was in very capable hands." He pulled her forward and placed a soft kiss on her cheek.

"Oh," Susan breathed. "It's my… I mean… that's what friends are for, right?"

"Right… but Celeste and I are forever grateful. And, am I to understand you'll continue deserving our gratitude during Celeste's recovery?"

"Well, yes, Susan has offered to accompany Celeste," Mitch stepped forward putting his hand on her shoulder, gently disengaging Susan from Ryan's fervent grip. "But we do have a few questions."

"I'm sure you do," Ryan perched on the bed, drew Celeste down to sit next to him and casually placed his hand on her knee. Celeste rested her head on his shoulder.

"Actually, I've done some research and as I understand it, as a medical professional, it should be easy to get approval for me to accompany Celeste, shouldn't it?" Susan didn't wait for a reply. "I have a letter of permission from my husband, we can get a letter from the doctor that she needs a health care professional to travel with her and all we need is your signature on the visa application. I'm sure your bosses can fast track both hers and mine. Then, you can be reassured that she's being taken care of when you're at work... at least until she's feeling better," Susan paused to take a breath and looked at Celeste and smiled.

"Well, looks like you two have thought of everything," Ryan chuckled. "Yes, I'm sure I can get the right paperwork submitted and have your visa approved quite quickly." Ryan turned to Mitch, "And, I assure you that Susan will be perfectly safe and will be treated like royalty during her visit to The Kingdom."

"See, there's nothing to worry about," Susan looped her arm through Mitch's and leaned in to give him a quick peck on the cheek. "Ryan is going to take care of everything."

The ward clerk arrived pushing an empty wheelchair. "Are you ready to go Mrs. Parker?"

"More than ready! But, do I really need that?"

"Your husband insisted... so, just enjoy the ride." The clerk smiled and guided Celeste into the chair.

"I'll push," Susan offered. "I might as well get into the role!"

Celeste reached back to pat Susan's hand. "Thanks," she smiled up at Susan. "Oh, and, Ryan and I thought it would be best if he went on ahead to Riyadh tomorrow, took care of all the paperwork and then we'll follow in a couple of days. Give us a chance to pack and for Ryan to start the search for Tamara. If she is there, we don't want to waste any more time... " her voice dwindled as Ryan threw her a glare.

The foursome rode the elevator down in silence and as they arrived at the opulent hospital lobby Ryan reached into his pocket for his keys. "Celeste, wait here, I'll get the car." He turned to Susan and Mitch. "It was nice meeting you... thank you again for all your help. I'll be in touch." He dismissed them, turned and breezed through the doors that automatically opened on his approach.

"Okay hon, we'll get going then," Susan squeezed Celeste's shoulders. "I'm going to get a work out in and I'll check with you a little later and see how the arrangements are coming along. I'm sure you guys will appreciate an evening alone. But, call in the meantime if you need anything at all."

"Thanks... I will," Celeste's voice cracked slightly and she cleared her throat. "I'm so glad you're coming with me."

"Me too... You know, now that I think of it, I'm sure Ryan's going to need a copy of my passport and probably a couple of photos, right?

Just let me know what you need and I can drop it off later along with any other documents he needs."

"I will." Celeste sighed.

"Hang in there," Mitch leaned over to kiss her cheek as Ryan pulled up.

"Let's go Celeste," Ryan called through the window. "We've got a lot to do and not much time... thanks again guys... really appreciate the help."

Mitch held Celeste's elbow and guided her to Ryan's Maserati and lowered her into the passenger seat. She gave him an appreciative glance as he made sure her skirt was inside and then closed the door for her.

"Suze, I'm not too sure about that guy," Mitch waved at the Parkers as they pulled away. He crossed his arms and turned to her. "Are you sure you want to do this?"

"Yes, I'm sure... he's just under a lot of pressure... give the guy a break why don't you? His daughter's missing and his wife's just had a nervous breakdown. Don't be so insensitive." Susan turned and walked briskly towards the visitor parking.

"Hey, now, hold on!" Mitch caught up and easily matched her stride. "I get that there's a lot going on for both of them but you've got to admit the guy's a bit of an arrogant asshole."

"I don't know... maybe," Susan stopped to fumble for her keys in her purse. "I guess I just want to give him the benefit of the doubt for now, okay?"

"Okay, okay… I'm just thinking about you," Mitch dangled her keys in front of her face. "I drove, remember?"

"You've got to stop jumping to conclusions about Tamara and don't get yourself all worked up again. It doesn't help matters." Ryan tried to control his voice. "She's going to turn up, you'll see. She's just rebelling against you suffocating her and treating her like a child. She's 18 now… it's good for her to start being independent."

"If that's true, it doesn't really make me feel any better," Celeste leaned her head against the car window and closed her eyes. "But I guess I'd rather believe that she's testing her independence instead of what my gut tells me."

"What does your gut tell you?"

"That she's been kidnapped."

"Jesus Celeste," Ryan floored the accelerator to pass another sports car that had sped up as he pulled into the left lane. "Don't be so melodramatic." He slammed on the breaks as the other driver passed on the right and then cut in front of him. "Fuck! The drivers here are nuts," Ryan gave the guy the finger.

Celeste grabbed his arm and pulled it down. "Don't do that... if he's Emirati he can report you and you could go to jail for that."

"I'd like to see him try. I have friends in high places too."

"You have to slow down anyway... our exit is coming up."

The other sports car had sped off into the distance blending in with the thousands of luxury vehicles jockeying for position on the 12-lane highway. Celeste watched the unending rows of skyscrapers flying by on either side. They flanked her like the walls of water that were held back for Moses and his followers, equally as ominous as it felt like they were about to come crashing in on her. *Hold it together girl... you'll find her.*

## *Chapter 19*

Ryan gripped his Chivas on the rocks as the company jet lifted off the runway. He raised the footrest of the overstuffed, black leather lazy boy and turned on the shiatsu massage that was built into the chair. It was a high-end piece of machinery and felt like there were actual fingers putting pressure on all the right sore spots. Even the headrest had a rhythmic, sliding impulse that ran up and down the length of his neck.

"Can I get you anything else sir?" The jet never went anywhere without at least one flight attendant, up to four depending on how many passengers there were. She was new and Ryan was irritated that she didn't know what he usually wanted... had to tell her to add two 'rocks' to his drink.

"Will you be having dinner this evening? We have either a filet mignon or roasted lamb."

"I'll have the lamb." Ryan preferred the lamb but it was rarely a choice, usually reserved for when a member of 'the family' was on board. He glanced over his shoulder towards the back of the plane to see if he could get a glimpse into the private cabin. He saw a swish of a white *dishdasha* as the sole occupant of the on board suite disappeared into the bathroom. The flight attendant pulled a red velvet curtain that separated the two cabins, cutting off his view.

Ryan shrugged his shoulders. It was probably someone he didn't know. The House of Saud, the ruling royal family of Saudi Arabia, was huge, with a couple of generations of princes and princesses, all direct descendants of Mohammad bin Saud and his three brothers. They were scattered throughout the Kingdom and paraded around like... well... royalty. And, it seemed as if many of them loved to escape to Dubai where the rules were loose and the sight of a man in a pristine white, crisply ironed *dishdasha* sitting at a hotel bar with an alcoholic drink in his hand was not out of the ordinary.

He didn't mind the hypocrisy... he was used to it. They could do whatever they wanted. He knew whoever was in the back was probably also enjoying a scotch. Ryan took another swig of his drink, sat back and tried to enjoy the massage. His neck and shoulders tightened into more knots as he thought about the pending meeting with the Minister. He was sure it was just a formality. The Minister probably wanted a project update and always preferred to hear from Ryan personally, face-to-face. It was how they usually communicated. In the Arab culture, email, Skype and even the telephone were unacceptable methods of doing business. It was okay for assistants and other underlings to use new technology as a means of setting up meetings and making offices run smoother and more efficiently but the real, high level communication must always be up close and personal. Ryan had also learned many years ago that at a first meeting, you never talk business. You drink coffee, talk about family, the horses, where you studied, recent travels... anything but the business proposal you have in mind. Once you've won their trust, you're golden and the projects come pouring in without even trying.

He smiled to himself and swirled his scotch around in its crystal 'old-fashioned' glass. Rydo Construction had made millions over the years from the Saudis and he knew he could convince the Minister he was still the best person to lead any high profile construction project in The Kingdom. He always knew that Donald was the real golden boy but after his death, Ryan had smoothly slid into the role, making sure there were no visible wrinkles or hiccups.

The only hiccup now was that he had to let Celeste and her pesky friend come to Riyadh. He was sure he had won Susan over but also knew that her husband was hesitant to let her come. Ryan would make sure it went smoothly and then send her back at the first opportunity. He reached for the envelope where he had slid it in the side pocket of his chair and thumbed through the documents. Copies of both women's passports, a copy of the letter from the doctor, Susan's CV and copy of her degree to prove her credentials and two passport-sized photos for each of them. He knew it was all a formality. His boss could fast track a visa for anyone without any of this but Ryan never made assumptions. You could fall out of favor much more easily than you gain it and he sensed his hold might be a little tenuous at the moment so had all the documents in order, including the letter from Mitch giving Susan permission to travel; accepting Ryan as her 'sponsor' in her capacity of medical travel aide for Celeste. Ryan would add a letter from himself confirming that he had hired Susan to care for his wife during her recovery from an undefined illness. Mental illness was still taboo in the Arab world and Ryan didn't want to bring attention to his wife's clinical depression. It would reflect badly on him and there would be speculation that he was not able to keep his wife happy. His Arab colleagues were lucky, he thought. They could easily replace a wife who was no longer useful, with a younger one and not even have to divorce the first one. He drifted off to sleep thinking that he should convert and how he could easily manage four wives.

## *Chapter 20*

Tamara wiped the steam from the mirror that had built up while she soaked in a soothing bath laced with aromatic lavender oil. She had succumbed to the luxury of her gilded cage and had decided to take advantage of her pampered confinement. *I don't get this kind of treatment at home...* she thought as she preened herself in the gold-rimmed make-up mirror. *Jesus, are those diamonds?* She peered closely at the stones embedded on the rim and raised her eyebrows at her reflection.

A knock on the door broke her away from her awe-struck pondering as she stood up and tightened the sash on the white satin robe Aliya had brought her. She stopped halfway to the door and exhaled loudly, realizing she wasn't able to open it from her side.

"Well, come in then... you've got the key," she plopped down on the end of the bed as Aliya slowly opened the door to peek inside.

"Oh good, you're up!" She swooped in, arms overflowing with black folds of material. "Here, get dressed and put this on." She handed her armload to Tamara.

"Why, what's up?" Tamara took the *abaya* and stroked the silky fabric and brought it up to her face.

"We're going shopping!" Aliya squealed. "Yusef says his father has given permission as long as he accompanies us and we don't take all day."

"Shopping? For what?" Tamara didn't care. She was already headed into the bathroom to change out of her pajamas. This would be the first time she had been out of the house... palace, really. She had mostly eaten in her room during her captivity but had joined the family for dinner a few times but knew she didn't have a chance of escaping with the armed guards on both the inside and outside of all the entrances she had seen. She had decided to take them at their word, that they were protecting her (she wasn't sure from what) and that her father would come get her as soon as he could.

"For dresses to wear to the wedding, of course," Aliya shooed her into the bathroom. "Hurry up or we won't have enough time!"

Tamara didn't have to be told twice. She threw her robe off, pulled on her jeans and t-shirt and slid the *abaya* over her head. She spun around as she re-entered the bedroom, feeling like a *Sheikha* with the rich folds swirling around her legs.

"You must put these on too," Aliya handed her a *shaylah* and veil to cover her hair and face.

Tamara stopped twirling. "Do I really have to? I'm covered just fine with this." She pulled on the sleeve.

"We must both cover our faces too," Aliya reached for the *shaylah* and delicately placed it on Tamara's head, tucking her blonde tendrils underneath. "I'll show you how the veil goes on when we get in the car."

Tamara knew there was no use arguing so she grabbed the leopard patterned Dolce & Gabbana purse Aliya had given her along with a few cosmetics. "Oh jeez," she stopped short. "I don't have any money."

Aliya's easy laugh was a soothing sound. "Oh we won't need money... we're going to the design house where our family has an open account. We can put yours on the account as well." She looped her arm casually through Tamara's and guided her along the hallway and down the wide, swooping staircase. She paused halfway down. The guards at the door were ushering in a tall, dark-haired visitor. He wore a smartly tailored suit that Tamara could tell was worth a pretty penny.

"Khalid, how nice to see you," Aliya continued down the remaining stairs, acknowledging him with a smile and a nod. Khalid locked his intense eyes on Tamara and opened his mouth to speak. Aliya cut him off before he could start. "I'm sorry but we can't stay to chat, we've got some serious business to take care of and I'm sure you're here to see father anyway," Aliya grinned and hurried Tamara past and out the door, giving a curt nod to the guards and guiding Tamara towards the white Cadillac Escalade limo parked in the driveway.

"Who's that?" Tamara asked. "He actually looks a little familiar to me... he's kinda hot for an old guy. Even the grey at his temples is pretty sexy."

"Shhh... don't say that so loud," Aliya looked behind them to make sure no one heard her. "He's my father-in-law's cousin. He's returned from the States recently after being away for many years. He was called back at the King's request to help at the Ministry of Commerce. His father is the minister there." She nudged Tamara down the last few steps and into the limo.

"Thank you Fahad," she murmured as the chauffeur closed the door behind them. She turned to her husband who was waiting inside. "Thank you for accompanying us Yusef. Did you already tell Fahad where we're going?"

Yusef finished the email he was sending from his phone, shut it off and turned his attention to his wife. "I assumed we were going to Ranya's design studio, right?" He patted her hand and turned to Tamara who was yanking on her veil trying to get it positioned so she could see. "You'll only have to wear that until we get into the studio. You can take it off once we're in," he sounded sympathetic. "I know it's bothersome and you're not used to it Tamara, but my father is very old-fashioned and since he's your temporary guardian while you're staying with us, you must cover." He smiled warmly and Tamara relaxed into the soft tan leather and accepted the bottle of water Yusef offered. She didn't bother to tell him that she had lived in Saudi until recently and had worn an *abaya* and *shaylah* before but, as an expat, had never been expected to wear a face cover.

"Excuse me sir, the studio? Is on King Fahd Road, yes?" Fahad called over his shoulder.

"Yes, almost to Cairo Square on the right side, remember? You took my mother there just last week." Yusef didn't wait for the driver's reply and pushed the button to close the window separating him from the occupants. "He's a bit nosey and I think he talks to the other drivers about our business too. He's not at all like his father but I guess it will take some time for him to adjust to our needs." Yusef shook his head and switched his phone back on while Aliya showed Tamara a few clever ways to wrap her head scarf so the veil would sit comfortably just under her eyes. Tamara watched out the window over Aliya's shoulder as the arid desert landscape gave way to the tall skyscrapers that flanked them on both sides, one more opulent than the next. She wondered which one her father worked in and when he would come to see her... or, if he really even knew where she was.

"*As-Salaam-Alaikum*, Mohammed," Karl, placed his hand on his chest and bowed slightly, then put it out to shake his cousin's. "I hope you are well."

"*Wa-Alaikum-Assalaam* cousin," Mohammed replied, gripped Karl's hand and pulled him in to kiss both cheeks. "Welcome back, Khalid. Come, let's sit and have coffee." Mohammed swept his arm towards the red velvet, gold tasseled cushions surrounding the centerpiece of the room - a large, Turkish silk rug, intricately hand-woven with camels and falcons. It was a piece of art that Karl thought should have been hung on the wall to admire, not spread on the floor to be trod upon.

"Thank you, it's good to be back." Karl followed Mohammed and took the cushion next to him and watched as Mohammed poured. He had actually missed the informal feel of the *majlis* while he worked in the U.S. where the boardrooms were way too stuffy and no one seemed to relax enough to just get to know one another before finalizing a deal. He shook his head silently pondering the differences between doing business in the Western world and the Middle East.

"I saw your daughter-in-law, Aliya, in the foyer but she seemed to be in a bit of a hurry." He took the cup Mohammed offered. "And, who was that beautiful blond little angel with her? Her face practically took my breath away... and those eyes! Like sparkling pale blue sapphires. I've never seen anything like it."

"Oh, just a friend of Aliya's from the International School... I think they studied there together. She's visiting while her parents are traveling... or something like that... Would you like her? I'm sure I could arrange it." Mohammed's mouth turned up in a suggestive smile and he raised his eyebrows.

"Good God no," Karl stared at Mohammed in disbelief. "She's far too young for me... and it doesn't look like she's the type to go for such an arrangement."

"As you wish, Khalid," Mohammed shrugged. "I guess your time in America has soured you to our ways." He sighed. "Well, if you change your mind, I'm sure she can be 'convinced'." He took a sip of his coffee. "Now, tell me how the convention centre project is going. I'm sure you have some initial impressions. Your father seems pleased with the progress. How is Ali working out as the project manager?"

"As far as I can tell, the project is a bit over schedule and seems to be over budget but I'll have a better idea once I take a closer look at the books," Karl swirled his coffee. "And, it seems like Ryan and Ali have some differences, mostly about the hours the laborers are working, but I'm sure they'll work them out."

"I'm sure they will," Mohammed stroked his chin. "You'll be going to your cousin's wedding this weekend, won't you? It'll give you a chance to catch up with any family you haven't seen since you've been back."

"Of course, I'll be there," Karl said. "I really can't stay long. I should get back to the office," he placed his cup on the low table in front of him. "I understand you have a package that you want me to bring to father?"

"Yes, it's in the foyer... please, finish your coffee first and tell me about your time in America."

## *Chapter 21*

Ryan sorted through a stack of papers, trying to find what he needed for his meeting with the Minister.

"Where the *hell* is the shipping manifest?" He swept the reams of paper onto the floor and hammered his desk.

He punched the intercom button. "Sheri, get Ali in here will ya. I'm meeting with the Minister in an hour and can't find anything," he growled.

"Right away sir," Sheri's efficient, unflappable voice came back. It was the one thing Ryan could always count on around the office. Sheri would never lose her cool and never failed to come through for him, whatever he needed. He smiled thinking about the last time she 'came through' for him and felt a brief twinge under the zipper of his pants. That would have to wait for now. He had to keep his head clear for this meeting and be prepared for any potential bombs the Minister might lob at him.

"Ryan?"

"Yes, Sheri."

"Just wanted to let you know your wife called and said she and her friend were about to

162

board the plane. Should I make arrangements to have them picked up and taken to the apartment?"

"That would be great, thanks... and, Sheri?"

"Yes?"

"Make sure the apartment is clean... you understand what I mean?"

"Of course. I'll take care of everything... how long will she be staying?" Ryan could hear a slight tinge of... what was that? Jealousy? He smirked to himself.

"Not long... now get me Ali, okay?"

"I already sent him an SMS and he should be here in five."

Ryan twisted his thick, white gold, diamond-encrusted wedding band. Celeste had thought it was a bit pretentious but Ryan liked the message it sent – *I'm rich and powerful so don't fuck with me!* The other meaning, that he was a married man, didn't seem to keep other women away. It seemed to make them even more persistent.

"I didn't know you had returned from your trip," Ali interrupted his thoughts, letting himself in without knocking, which made Ryan's blood boil. He had very specific rules of engagement for his staff. This was his domain and he insisted that anyone knocked before entering or be announced first by Sheri.

"I didn't hear you knock," Ryan ground out through clenched teeth. He didn't like Ali but the Ministry had appointed him as the project foreman and as a contractor, Ryan had no control over whom they assigned in that role. He also knew Ali was vying for a higher position. But Rydo Construction was Ryan's company and he'd be damned if this slimy, do-gooder would get anywhere beyond being a lackey to him. He also knew Ali was the only college educated one in his family... he bragged about it constantly. He was probably qualified for the job but that didn't make Ryan like him any better. He didn't trust him, as his loyalties were elsewhere. Ali's parents had been working for some cousin of the Minister's since Ali was a kid and they had vouched for him with the Minister to get the job.

"Oh sorry, I didn't knock... Did you need me for something?" Ali sauntered across the room and dropped onto the couch and reached for the coffee urn and helped himself.

"What the f..." Another one of Ryan's rules... no one is served coffee before the boss. "Ali, what the hell are you doing? I didn't invite you in here for a coffee chat... I need you to find the latest shipping manifest from Italy. I know that the marble arrived, didn't it? But, the paperwork's not here. I'm sure I left it on my desk." Ryan walked slowly toward Ali and stopped by the arm of the couch, towering over him. "I also can't find the sketches for the Chihuly designs that will be the center-piece of the lobby and the *majlis*." He glared down at him. "I'm meeting with the Minister today and I need those documents."

"I think I did see them on your desk... I decided to use your office while you were away," Ali looked at the papers strewn across the floor.

"They're probably somewhere in that mess." His arm made a sweeping arc in the direction of the papers.

Ryan clenched his fists at his sides to keep from grabbing Ali by the scruff of the neck and tossing him out of his office. "Why weren't you working from the site?"

"I had several meetings here so it was more convenient," Ali stood up and walked a few paces, putting more distance between them. "I did come across something quite interesting." He ran his fingers down the blade of the sword held by the full-sized, black jade Samurai warrior statue that Ryan had brought back from a trip to Japan. The statue was taller and broader than Ali, closer to Ryan's height and build.

"Oh, and what might that be?" Ryan picked up Ali's cup and dumped the contents into the sink of the wet bar.

"A statement for a numbered account in Zurich, at least I think it was anyway... with what appeared to be a very large sum of money."

Ryan could feel the pulse in his throat thrumming like a bullfrog as he turned slowly to face Ali. "I'd say you must have been imagining things."

"No, I don't think so," Ali walked around to the back of the couch and smoothed the hair that had been ruffled by the breeze that came in through the open door of the balcony scattering the papers further.

Ryan glanced out at the camel-colored sky that was becoming darker and thick with dust by the second and knew a *shamal* was brewing. "I think you need to forget about it and help me find the documents I'm looking for," Ryan said as he continued towards Ali.

"I think you've been padding the accounts and skimming money..." Ali was behind Ryan's desk looking at him with wild eyes. "And, I think the Minister knows..." he continued quickly as Ryan bore down on him. "And, he has your daughter!"

Ryan stopped. "You don't know what are you talking about."

"My brother works as a chauffer for the Minister's cousin... used to work here cleaning the offices," Ali paused and swallowed, gathering courage.

"Go on." Every nerve-ending in Ryan's body burned like hot pokers under his skin as his mind raced to grasp what Ali was saying. Did his brother work for the same family the parents had all those years? So, the Minister did know... but how? He'd been so careful all this time.

"Fahad, my brother, took some of the family members shopping yesterday and recognized your daughter from that picture," Ali pointed to the family portrait Ryan had on his bookshelf next to his prized copy of *Sun Tsu - The Art of War*. "He said she asked where you were and when she could see you." Ali threw back his shoulders like he had triumphed.

166

"And, what exactly do you propose to do with this information," Ryan closed the remaining space between them and could see the drops of sweat forming on Ali's forehead.

"I won't do anything as long as you take care of my needs." Ali crossed his arms over his chest putting up a thin barrier.

"What might those be?" Ryan's voice lowered to a menacing tone. He realized now that Ali had probably been spying on him for a while now.

"I want the position of VP of operations for Rydo Construction that has opened up and a $1 million signing bonus."

Ryan laughed out loud. "Is that all?" He gripped the back of his leather chair.

"And, I want you to give the workers back their day off."

"And, what if I don't?"

"I'll tell Karl and maybe even your wife... she doesn't know, does she?" Ali smiled like he held a royal flush.

"Well, I'll tell you what I'm going to give you." Ryan lunged at him and gripped Ali's throat in his shovel-sized hand, which almost wrapped around the full diameter of his neck. "I'm going to give you a free trip to hell!" In a rage Ryan propelled Ali several feet across the office, through the open sliding glass doors and to the edge of the balcony 20 stories above the ground. The wind had kicked up a sand blasting frenzy and was howling like the demons of Hades had come personally to accept Ryan's gift. Ali's feet were dangling and he was kicking out at Ryan as he tightened his grip on Ali's throat. Ryan heaved him effortlessly over the balcony and watched him disappear into the swirling sand, his screams swallowed up by the raging storm.

Ryan backed up into his office, tucked his shirt back into his waistband and brushed the dust off. He slid the door closed to block out the airborne grains of sand that stung his face like a swarm of mosquitos at dusk.

He turned to survey the mess of his office as Karl swung open the door while knocking with one knuckle.

"Hey Ryan, sorry for barging in but Sheri's not at her desk.... Holy shit... what happened here?"

"Oh... shit... I... nothing," Ryan stammered trying to gather his wits. "This *shamal* kicked up out of no where and the door was open so it blew the papers off my desk," he finished as he ran both hands through his hair. He glanced down at his desk and spied the edge of the manifest he had been looking for sticking out from under his keyboard.

"For the love of Allah Ryan, don't you have to meet with the Minister today?" Karl stooped down to help gather the papers scattered across the room. "I thought I would stop in and see if you want me to come with you and to return these." He handed Ryan the sketches for the glass sculptures.

"I asked Ali to see them while you were gone, I hope you don't mind."

"No, that's fine." Ryan took them and put them on his desk.

"They're really spectacular," Karl offered. "I saw the Chihuly exhibit when it was in Miami and it was amazing. I was also at the opening of the Atlantis Hotel on The Palm in Dubai... the piece Chihuly did for their lobby is exquisite. Good call on this one Ryan."

"Uh, yeah... thanks."

"Where is Ali? I thought he was coming to see you."

"No... ah, actually he was here but I went out to the supply room to get something... and when I came back he had left." Ryan sat down at his desk busying himself. "I don't know what's going on with him but he seemed really upset about something. I know he thinks we're working the laborers too hard but time is money, you know."

"Yeah Ryan, we do need to talk about that but it can wait," Karl sat in the visitor's chair across from Ryan. "I wanted to ask you about something else though."

"Hmmm... what's that? You know, I've really got to get going Karl or I'll be late... I'm sure your father will keep me waiting an hour but I still need to be there at the appointed time. You never know with these guys, right?" Ryan winked at Karl, who was technically one of 'those guys' but after all his years in the U.S. had more of a Westernized work

169

ethic... had even replaced his *dishdasha* with a black suit, although he often put a *bisht*, a traditional Arab cloak, over his suit if he had business with the Minister or other important official.

"I just wondered what's going on with Celeste... is she okay? I haven't seen her in years... actually since Donald died..." his voice trailed off as Ryan looked up at him.

"She's fine... just over-tired and a little off-balance trying to set up the house in Dubai by herself, but she'll be okay. Oh, and thanks for your help getting the visa fast-tracked for her and her friend. I guess your friends are in higher places than mine." He stood up dismissing Karl. "Don't worry, I can handle this one on my own but I'll let you know how it goes."

"I'm sure you can... I just think it's strange. I have been involved in the update sessions since I got back but when I spoke with my father this morning he suggested my presence wasn't actually necessary, unless you felt it was important to have me present."

"It makes sense for us to 'divide and conquer' ... he knows you've got other projects to oversee for him as well and that I've got things under control with the conference center." Ryan reached for the door. He wanted Karl to stop prying. He wasn't sure how far he could trust him either. They had drifted apart after university. Karl had stayed in the States while Ryan and Donald had started up Rydo Construction and began working on projects in the Middle East, Asia and Africa. He knew, however, that Donald had kept in touch.

"Hold up a second," Karl was right behind Ryan and put his hand on his elbow. "You also mentioned some problem with your daughter. Is everything okay?"

"Of course... thanks for asking... she just wanted to get away for a few days with friends and Celeste got herself all worked up about it because she didn't tell her," Ryan waved him off. "I've got to get going. I'll let you know when the meeting's finished."

"Good luck then... and, don't forget, we have the presentation at the Chamber tomorrow. Everyone is eager for an update on the grand opening. We need to schedule that soon, right?"

"Yes, of course... should be able to do that next week. We'll just build the excitement and let everyone know they're getting an invitation soon. That'll cool their jets."

"Whatever you say, it's your project. Call me when you get back from the meeting. And, be careful. That's a brutal sand storm... but it should blow by in a few minutes. I don't think it was supposed to last long."

Ryan mumbled a reply and punched his driver's number into his phone as he strode towards the elevator and Karl headed in the opposite direction to his office.

"I'm on my way down. Have the car out front. We're going to the Ministry," he snapped the order into his phone then slapped the case closed and cursed under his breath. He was starting to think he knew why Karl hadn't been invited to this meeting. A feeling of dread started building in the pit of his stomach like a growling Rottweiler on the other side of a chain link fence.

By the time Ryan arrived at the Ministry, he was wound up so tight his neck muscles could have snapped. The traffic on the Airport Road was stopped for more than 20 minutes, while work vehicles cleared sand from a runway following the storm and an Airbus A380 with the Royal Families' insignia waited to take off. Ryan watched it careen down the runway with his teeth clenched as the extra minutes he had planned to mentally prepare himself in the Minister's outer office were frittered away.

He took a deep, cleansing breath like he was about to dead lift 300 pounds, and grabbed the solid crystal, falcon-shaped door handle, which Ryan knew was designed by Swarovski since he had sourced it himself. He pushed through the smoked double glass door and delivered his most brilliant smile to the Minister's assistant, and gatekeeper, sitting behind a large, solid oak desk. Her desktop gleamed with a newly polished sheen and had only a computer and a phone message pad gracing its surface. Behind her on the wall were two large portraits - one of the King and one of the Minister.

"Good morning Miriam," he greeted her. "How are you today?"

"Good morning Mr. Parker, the Minister is waiting for you." She stood up, gathered the black folds of her *abaya* and swept them off her chair. She floated by him and motioned for him to follow. Ryan's heart pounded in his chest as he was escorted into the lion's den. He was livid he hadn't arrived earlier but he had to shake it off. He couldn't show any weakness... never had, never would.

"*As-Salaam-Alaikum* Minister," Ryan bowed and put his hand on his heart, waiting for the Minister to put his hand out first as was customary.

"*Wa-Alaikum-Assalaam* Ryan, please have a seat." The Minister waved his arm towards the low, elaborately cushioned *majlis* where he held all his informal meetings and did not extend his hand for Ryan to shake. He smiled but it was more like a desert viper ready to strike than a welcoming, friendly smile.

Ryan nodded his head and lowered himself onto the seat next to where the Minister was settling. A low side table separated them by about three feet. He hated the traditional Arab seating arrangement. The chairs were elevated only about a foot off the ground, too low for his exceptionally tall build and there were too many pillows that were always in the way. At least they weren't just cushions right on the floor like some of the others had in their offices. He preferred a modern boardroom where he felt more like an equal. There was one right next to Bashir's office, but Ryan knew the Minister was old-fashioned and favored the *majlis*. He wondered if Karl would replace his father in the Ministry. There had been speculation that was the reason he was back from the States.

The Minister was busying himself rearranging the *ghutra* covering his head, making sure it was perfectly straight under the *agal*, the black rope that encircled the top of the white fabric that held it firmly in place. He stirred his coffee with a sugar stick and still hadn't spoken. Ryan knew he must wait until his boss spoke first. He watched as Miriam poured Arab coffee from an ornate silver urn with an elegant curving spout into a demi-tasse and held it out to him. Ryan shifted his weight and crossed his ankles together so his knees weren't up under his chin. He leaned forward and accepted the cup Miriam handed to him. It wouldn't have been polite, actually was not advisable, to decline even though he was not at all fond of the liquid it held... tasted to him like weak, swampy swill. He smiled and thanked her and she silently glided out of the room and closed the door behind her.

## *Chapter 22*

"Take the worried look off your face sweetheart, everything's going to be fine," Susan put her hand on Mitch's cheek and rubbed her thumb across his brow, willing away the concerned dents between his eyes. "And, besides, check this out." She waved her hand towards the Gulf Stream jet that would take her and Celeste to Riyadh. "We're being treated like royalty."

Mitch couldn't deny that, as he looked at the red carpet that ran from the exit of the private lounge they had come through, out onto the tarmac right up to the boarding stairs of the aircraft.

"I'm just glad my Emirates ID allowed me to come all the way with you guys. If they can trust me on the tarmac wandering around a triple-seven, they can certainly trust me around here, right?" Mitch tried to make light of the situation but the gnawing in the pit of his stomach made him wary.

"I told Ryan we wouldn't mind flying commercial but he said Karl insisted we take the jet," Celeste said as she looped her arm through Susan's.

"Evening ladies," the plane's captain and a flight attendant stood waiting at the foot of the stairs in starched navy blue uniforms with crisp white shirts. "I'm Paul Radford, I'll be your captain tonight and this is Sylvie, your flight attendant. Please come aboard. You can leave your bags here and we'll take care of securing them in the luggage hold.

Mitch shook the captain's hand. "You take care of my wife now," he smiled.

"You won't be coming with us?"

"No, not this time. I've got to get to my own gate... operating a flight to Bangkok in about an hour." Mitch pulled Susan aside and with both hands on her shoulders, looked at her straight in the eye, looking for any sign of uneasiness or doubt. "You sure you want to do this?"

"Of course I'm sure... can't let Celeste go by herself and I'm just the woman for the job! Now go do your flight and I'll send you an SMS when we get settled. We can even Skype tomorrow if you want."

"Okay, but it worries me you don't actually have a return ticket." He leaned over and kissed her on the cheek. He'd rather have given her a proper kiss but he knew the rule of no public displays of affection. Even the kiss on the cheek could have been considered offensive if an Emirati had been close by and saw them.

"Thanks for letting her come with me Mitch," Celeste extended her hand. "I can really use her help."

"Don't mention it," said Mitch. "Besides, I couldn't stop her if I wanted to. You guys take care of each other okay?" He watched as they both headed up the stairs and turned around at the door. Susan blew him a kiss and Mitch waved. He waited until the door was secured and the stairs drove away before he turned and headed back into the terminal, his hands shoved deep into his the pockets of his uniform pants.

The ladies got settled into their comfy chairs each with a welcome glass of champagne in their hands. "Cheers to a successful mission... getting you healthy and finding Tamara," said Susan clinking Celeste's glass.

"That's certainly a toast I could support," Celeste agreed and set her glass down without taking a sip.

"Oh right... Sorry. It's probably better you don't drink that with the meds you're on. One glass would be okay but that always tastes like another, doesn't it?" Susan put her own glass aside. "Now, who's Karl again? You may have told me but I don't remember."

"I guess he's technically Ryan's boss," Celeste pondered. "But he and Ryan and my late husband Donald went to Harvard together. Donald and Karl kept in touch after they graduated but I haven't heard from him or seen him since Donald went missing." Celeste opened the packaging on the blanket the flight attendant had left on her seat and spread it out over her legs. "He lived in the U.S. until maybe a month ago and now he's in Saudi working for his father who's the Minister of Industry and Commerce or some such thing, for the Saudi government. Ryan says he liaises with all the construction contractors, him included."

"Hmmm... it'll be nice for you to reconnect with him then," Susan said.

"Well, maybe," Celeste picked at a loose thread. "Ryan has always been a bit jealous of Karl so I'm not sure he'll be inviting him to dinner or anything."

"Well he'd be a great ally in making some inquiries about Tamara's whereabouts," Susan speculated out loud. "He's obviously well connected."

"I agree, but we'll have to be careful talking about it around Ryan... he's so convinced Tamara just went off with some friends. I can't believe he's not more concerned." Celeste twisted a napkin around her finger. "He's so eager for her to 'toughen up' as he calls it and be independent. You know, his mother died when he was about 12 years old.... " Celeste's voice faded to a whisper. "I'm sorry Susan, I'm not sure I should be telling you this. Ryan's such a private man. I'm sure there are still things about him I don't even know."

"That's okay hon, I won't say anything," Susan stroked her hand and took the shredded napkin from her. "I can see there's more... you can tell me," Susan said gently.

"Well, I guess so... It's a horrible story," she paused and took a deep breath. "His father had given him a hunting rifle for his birthday... they would go duck-hunting together... anyway... Ryan was cleaning it in his bedroom and his mother came in to tell him he should be cleaning it in the garage so he didn't get grease all over his bed," Celeste swallowed. "She grabbed the barrel of the rifle and apparently it went off and ..."

"Oh my God, Celeste! Jeee-sus, no wonder he's so serious all the time. That's not something you ever get over," Susan handed Celeste a fresh Kleenex.

"The way he told the story to me sounded so unbelievable but what upset me more was how detached he was when he told the story... in pretty vivid detail." Celeste took a deep breath and continued. "Of course, his father couldn't be consoled and couldn't stand to look at his own son. Even though he didn't press any charges he sent Ryan away to live with relatives."

"Has he had counseling?" Susan asked.

"Are you kidding? That would be a sign of weakness... he doesn't want anyone to know that I've had counseling or that I have problems with depression."

"Celeste, I'm going to say something now as a mental health nurse, not as your friend, okay?"

"Okay...?" Celeste wasn't sure she wanted to hear what was coming.

"If Ryan has never seen anyone about this part of his past, he could be suffering from PTSD, Post Traumatic Stress Disorder... although it wasn't called that back then and it's not just war vets who can suffer from it. Ryan's denial is most likely affecting the way he communicates with you and sometimes he may treat you in a way that triggers your breakdowns. Has he ever been violent with you?"

"No, absolutely not," Celeste sat up and pulled her hand from Susan's. "If anything, he's been terribly patient with me. I have a lot to be grateful for... he was right there for me when Don went missing."

"I know, I know, shh shh... I didn't mean to upset you," Susan fixed the cushion behind Celeste's head and she leaned back on it.

"I'm sorry... I realize you're trying to help. It's all so messed up and you've been a real gem. I guess together Ryan and I are like a Molotov cocktail waiting to explode." She shook her head and her eyes welled up with tears. *And you don't know the half of it* she thought almost feeling guilty for dragging Susan into her chaotic world but desperately needing a friend.

# *Chapter 23*

The Minister finished stirring the sugar into his coffee, sat back and took a sip. "Ah, Miriam makes the best Arabian coffee, don't you think?"

"She sure does," Ryan choked down another sip in solidarity and waited to see what direction the conversation would go.

"So, I understand your family will be joining you... I thought you had re-located them to Dubai."

"Yes, they are living in Dubai now but my wife just needed a break so she and a care giver are coming. She was recently in the hospital and needs some time to recuperate. My daughter is staying behind in Dubai with friends."

"Really? Well, I hope your wife's recovery is uneventful." He reached for the files Ryan had placed on the table between them. "So, what do you have for me? Is everything on track for completion? We are preparing the guest list for the grand opening and must also finalize a date before the end of the month so plans can proceed. We need a firm date so we can confirm the Cirque du Soleil who will perform at the opening. This new facility will be the showpiece of the Kingdom and, as it will bear the name of the King, nothing can go wrong."

"Of course, Minister. There's no need to worry... everything's under control and, after a few minor set backs, we're back on target for completion."

Ryan relaxed a bit realizing the meeting really was just a progress report on the project. He thought about the multi-purpose conference/ convention behemoth he was building that also included a coliseum-esque section where the King would hold quarterly public meetings, like a traditional *majlis*. His 'people' would be invited to send questions and concerns in advance and a select few (only of the male persuasion) would be chosen to present these to the Consultative Council, and the King, in person. The audience would watch the proceedings as a demonstration of how those appointed by the King represented the people's best interests. The 150 council members were assigned to committees that addressed issues such as education, health, culture, foreign affairs, security and human rights. Women would be allowed to attend but only as spectators and only if accompanied by a male relative. When it wasn't being used for official business, it would be the site of world-class performances of symphonies, ballets and operas, carefully selected by the censorship committee to ensure appropriate subject matter.

"We're just doing the final touches like the marble wall and the glass sculptures that will be the center-piece of both of the main entrances, the *majlis* and the convention center. The sketches are there," Ryan indicated the file the Minister was holding.

"Yes, I see... I assume there are no others like them anywhere else in the world?"

"Absolutely... they'll be the biggest sculptures Chihuly has ever done. He'll be here next week to oversee the installation himself."

"Excellent... I would like to meet him when he comes. Make that happen."

"No problem," Ryan gritted his teeth to stop from suggesting that Miriam should be making those types of arrangements. He didn't have time to make appointments for other people. He was busy overseeing the construction of the biggest, most spectacular facility in the Kingdom, probably in the Middle East. It would even trump Ferrari World in Abu Dhabi. He knew the lead contractor on that project and couldn't wait to rub his face in it as Ryan had beat him out on the bid for the conference centre.

"And, Ryan... we had some disturbing news just before you arrived today."

"Oh?"

"Yes, your project foreman was found dead on the backside of your office building. Actually, the side your office faces I believe. It was difficult to identify him at first as he apparently fell from several stories. They had to check the ID in his wallet."

"That's terrible," Ryan slowly placed his cup on the table and leaned forward, lacing his fingers together to keep them from shaking. "What happened?"

"We don't know for sure, but we believe he fell from one of the balconies on the upper floors... or he was pushed..." the Minister looked at Ryan and raised his eyebrows. "Only the executive offices have balconies." The Minister rose from his chair and towered over Ryan, who was still seated. "I hope that won't effect the timing of the project's completion." He continued by Ryan, the folds of his *ghutra* brushing across the top of Ryan's head, and made his way back to his desk. He motioned to the visitor chair.

Ryan seethed inside, feeling like a puppet, but still reacted to the yanked strings and stiffly unfolded himself to his full height. He smoothed his hair, threw his shoulders back, then calmly took a deep breath and sauntered over and took the appointed seat across the desk from the Minister. He would regain control of this conversation.

"You know, I was worried about him," Ryan crossed his arms and shook his head. "I think the demands of the job were too much for him... he seemed to be at a breaking point the last time I saw him. I told him he should take a day off." Ryan thought that was a nice touch... play the sympathy card.

"Is that so? Well, as his boss, you would notice, wouldn't you?" The Minister pulled another thick file out from under a pile and started flipping through it. Ryan thought he recognized the logos of several of his suppliers on top of the some of the pages. "You know his family has worked for my cousin for many years. It's going to be quite devastating for them. It's going to be a difficult phone call to make. His brother still works for Mohammed... my cousin... and his father worked for them and his father before him. You could say they're almost like family."

Ryan knew that was a stretch. They would never consider an employee 'like family' but there was often a sense of loyalty on both sides when they were getting what they wanted and one generation of servants trained the next.

"Yes, I did understand there was a connection... that he came from your referral," Ryan's insides squirmed like his intestines were trying to digest a batch of earthworms. "Please send them my condolences."

"Oh I think you'll be able to give them yourself at my niece's wedding this weekend, which you will attend with your wife, as I understand she's here now... and maybe make an apology to Mohammed for driving Ali to his death." Bashir didn't look up from the papers in his hands. "I just hope my cousin doesn't take it out on Tamara.... That is your daughter's name, isn't it?" He looked up, folded his hands on top of the file and smiled.

"Yes.... That's her name," Ryan put his hands on the desk to steady himself. "What do you know about Tamara?"

"Oh, only that she's been a guest of my cousin's for a little over a week now and seems to be settling in quite nicely."

"What is she doing there and what exactly do you mean 'settling in'," Ryan's voice trembled with a combination of anger and fear. "How did she get here? I demand to see her!" Ryan stood up and hammered on the desk.

"Sit down!" The Minister growled. "You are in no position to make demands. Actually, there is much explaining to do. And, until these are explained to my satisfaction, Tamara will remain a guest of the Family." He pushed the file towards Ryan.

Ryan's heart dropped into his stomach as he slowly opened the file and pulled out the first paper. His insides clenched and he felt like the floor was about to open up and swallow him whole. It was the original invoice for the marble, showing $1 million less than the copy he had just shown the Minister and that he had already submitted for payment into his company's account. All sub-contractors were paid through Rydo Construction and the Ministry paid Ryan. He flipped quickly through the stack of papers that went back at least a year. He tried to swallow the bile that rose in his throat and threatened to spew forth.

"Where did you get these," he stammered. "I don't believe they're accurate. I'll have Sheri prepare copies of the correct invoices and bring them right over." He dug in his pocket for his phone, glanced over where he had been sitting and spied it on the cushion.

"Don't bother, these are directly from the companies and I've been assured these are the correct numbers... what each of them were paid for services rendered or products and supplies sold."

Ryan could feel the color draining from his face. He tried to calculate the amount of money he had skimmed over the years but the numbers just swam around in his brain, refusing to tabulate. He had been getting away with it for so long he always thought they were too stupid to notice and too stinking rich to care. No one had ever audited Rydo's books before although he kept two sets of books. He had worked his ass off for these arrogant bastards and deserved to be paid for basically giving his life to them for the past 20 years.

"Well, your excellency," Ryan switched gears to a more respectful tone. "I do have to add a fee for my oversight. And, I'm sure you would agree *our* work over the years has been impeccable." It was time to conjure up the memory of his dead partner, whom 'the Family' was always closer to than they were to Ryan. Hell, it was always understood, even when Donald was around, that a sub-contractor's bill would be marked up... but of course the expectation was about a 10-15 percent mark-up, not 100. He hoped that fact would escape the Minister's notice. And, he could certainly direct the attention and suspicion towards Ali.

"You know I had counted on Ali to handle the billing for this project... thought I could give him more responsibility," Ryan shook his head. "I guess I should have watched him more closely."

"Hmmm... indeed. However, before Ali met his untimely death, he had been gathering a few documents for me, with the help of your lovely assistant, and the 'mark-ups' as you call them, are staggering."

Ryan closed his eyes and pinched the bridge of his nose. He pictured the file with the information on his shell company in Singapore and the numbered account in Zurich he had put in his desk drawer meaning to put it back in the safe a few days before. Had Ali found it? Did the Minister have it? He had left abruptly when Celeste wound up in the hospital and forgot about it. *Fucking Celeste!* And, he couldn't believe Sheri would betray him. *Bitch!* He would take great pleasure in firing her ass.

"Sir, I will get to the bottom of this... and will deal with Sheri too..." Ryan began but the Minister cut him off.

"Don't worry, we've found another more important role for Miss Sheri," the Minister said, seeming to enjoy Ryan's predicament and even reading his thoughts. "She will join my office staff and work with Miriam on special assignments. Her first one will be the grand opening of the King's Community and Convention Center." He picked at some non-existent dirt under a perfectly manicured fingernail. "And, from now on, you'll be working from the site so you won't need an executive assistant anymore. Now, I have another meeting shortly so please leave. We'll continue this at a later date." He picked up the phone and started dialing.

"What about my daughter?" Ryan leaned onto the desk.

"Don't worry," he glared at Ryan as he waited for his party on the other end to answer. "We'll be keeping her safe until this 'misunderstanding' can be worked out." He swiveled his chair around to face the window.

Ryan was dismissed.

## *Chapter 24*

*Shit… they did have Tamara!* Ryan tried to maintain his composure as he walked past Miriam's desk.

"Mr. Parker," she called after him. "Here are your invitations to the wedding," she held out three envelopes. "I believe you will need one for yourself for the men's reception and two for your wife and her friend for the women's. Is that correct?"

"Uh, yes… right, thank you Miriam." He took the envelopes from her, turned on his heel and left quickly before she could delay him any further. He had to pull his thoughts together and figure out what to do. *They still need me to finish this project and they wouldn't harm Tamara or Celeste… would they?*

"Fuck me," Ryan swore under his breath as he punched the elevator button and texted his driver he was on his way down. He'd have to go to the apartment next and make sure Susan and Celeste were settled in and comfortable. The last thing he needed was for Celeste's friend to be suspicious and tell her husband that anything was out of place. What they needed was some spa and shopping excursions to keep them busy and the wedding would be a distraction too. Thank God the men and women were separated at Arab weddings. He could take care of business and not worry about Celeste overhearing any sensitive conversations. He just had to figure out how to convince her that Tamara was fine and not to go poking their noses where they didn't belong.

"This place is spectacular," Susan took in the opulence of Ryan's apartment, from the crystal chandelier in the foyer to the original oil paintings in the living room. "Oh my God, is that a Monet?" Susan walked across the marble floor and dropped her purse on the couch. She leaned in to look closely at the painting that hung above it. "Definitely his signature and if it's not an original, it's a damned good copy." She whistled appreciatively.

"Ah, you know art," Celeste followed her into the living room. "It is a beautiful piece, isn't it? And, I can assure you it's the real McCoy. One thing about these guys is, they don't 'do' fake."

"Well, I took a few art history classes as electives in university to balance out all the hard-core science I had to take." Susan wandered around the apartment, admiring more of the artwork on the walls and the sculptures adorning every corner. "And, Mitch and I have spent a fair bit of time exploring museums and galleries in Paris and Rome... as an airline employee he gets some great travel perks."

"Sounds lovely," Celeste sat on the piano bench. "I'd love to see more of Europe. She sighed. "Ryan works so hard and travels for business so much, when he does take time off it's not enough to really go anywhere and he'd rather relax than get on another plane."

"Hmmm... I can understand that," Susan picked up her purse. "What I'd like to see now is the bathroom... and, wouldn't mind a hot bath. Is that ok? I'm sure you could use one too."

"Of course. Your room is down the hallway, the last one on the right and there's an on-suite," Celeste pointed in the direction of the bedrooms. "There should be everything you need but just give me a shout if not."

"Ok, will do," Susan answered as she peered down the long corridor. "But I'm not sure you'll hear me... that's a long way down." She laughed as she pulled her 'wheel aboard' suitcase behind her and disappeared down the hallway.

Celeste knew Ryan would be arriving soon... he promised he wouldn't be working late. She needed to see him and needed to talk about finding Tamara. She hoped he would be in a good mood. She poured herself a glass of water and shook one of her pills from the bottle she kept in her purse. They seemed to be keeping her anxiety at bay so she gratefully swallowed it down as she heard Ryan's key in the lock. She took a quick look at her reflection in the mirror, smoothed her hair back and ran her fingers under her eyes to remove the smudge of mascara that inevitably appears a few hours after application. She could hear the water running in Susan's bathroom and the strains of the Rolling Stones' 'I can't get no satisfaction' floating down the hallway. *She must have seen the iPod speaker dock and plugged in her iPhone.*

She put on a big smile as Ryan entered the apartment. Her smile faded as she took in his stormy expression.

"Hello darling, can I get you a drink?"

"Hell yes... where's your friend?"

"She's taking a bath... she'll be out soon," Celeste poured scotch from the decanter on the silver tray on the sideboard. "Want to talk about it?"

"Not really..." he reached for the drink Celeste held out to him and took a long swig. He set his briefcase down in the hall and in two long strides was in the living room sitting in the large armchair in the corner next to the baby grand piano. "Aren't you having one?" He gestured towards the mahogany drink cart.

"No, I don't think I should with these new pills I'm on... maybe a glass of wine at dinner," Celeste sat opposite him on the couch. "I haven't had a chance to check the grocery situation... should I cook or shall we order in?"

"There's not much so I guess we'll have to order in then. You can take my driver and go for groceries tomorrow after he takes me to the office."

"Ok." Celeste waited.

"And, we're going to a wedding this weekend so you might as well get him to take you two shopping for a dress as well." He reached into the pocket of his jacket slung over the back of the armchair and handed her the invitations.

"But, we just arrived..." she began.

"Don't argue with me. It's a command performance Celeste... the Minister's niece is getting married."

"Oh... well, I guess it'll be nice to show Susan what a traditional Arab wedding is like." Celeste took a deep breath and leaned forward. "Ryan, I think we need to talk about Tamara... surely you're worried about her too?"

"What the hell are you talking about? I told you there was no need to worry... Didn't I tell you I spoke with her?"

"What do you mean you spoke with her?" Celeste's voice rose an octave. "Where is she? Is she ok?"

"Calm the fuck down Celeste... I can't deal with your dramatics," Ryan stood up and Celeste cowered. He poured himself another scotch and perched on the bar stool under the kitchen pass through. "It's no wonder she doesn't want to talk to you."

"What do you mean? Where is she Ryan?" Celeste clenched her teeth, trying to hold it together while her insides roiled like a kettle over an open fire.

"Like I expected, she's staying with some friends in Dubai... she just needs her space Celeste... she said you've been acting so crazy she needed to get away. She said to tell you she's fine and she'll see you when you get back."

"Which friend? Give me the number." Celeste stood up and crossed her arms.

"I told you, she doesn't want to talk to you." Ryan took another drink.

"I don't care what she told you to tell me, I'm her mother and I need to talk to her to make sure she's ok... and talk to the parents where she's staying." Celeste's voice evened out as she gained the confidence of a protective mother. "Ryan, we barely know her friends in Dubai, let alone their parents. Is it Heidi she's staying with?"

"Yeah, that name sounds familiar."

"For Christ sake Ryan, can't you act a little more like a father? Why didn't you ask more questions? I don't think it's Heidi... I spoke with Karen, her mother, before I left and she hadn't seen Tamara. Now, what friend is it? Did Tamara call from her cell phone or from the friend's home phone? I haven't been able to get through on her cell all week." Celeste reached for Ryan's phone but he snatched it off the counter before she could get it.

"Celeste, get a grip... you're not calling. It's this interrogation you always launch into that she's sick of... as a matter of fact, I'm sick of it too." He slammed down his glass and reached for his briefcase.

"Where are you going... we're not finished," Celeste tried to block his way. "Ryan, don't you dare leave... I demand you give me that number. I know you have it in your phone. Why won't you let me see?" She reached again for the phone Ryan was gripping and he pushed her hand away.

"Give me the phone," she growled. "She's *my* daughter... not yours!" The words were out of her mouth before she could stop them. She didn't see his huge fist coming at her as it landed full-force, slamming into her eye and half her cheek. She stumbled backwards and fell onto the sofa. Her hand flew to her face as she looked up at him, shocked and confused. He had finally crossed that fine line and Celeste just knew she had pushed him there.

"You don't think I knew that?" He advanced on her slowly, with a menacing growl. The music from Susan's bathroom had gotten louder as Mick belted out 'Start Me Up'. "You think I'm an idiot? I know I've been raising Donald's daughter for the past 18 years... I have his business, his wife and his daughter. Just as I planned it."

"What? I-I don't understand... planned what?"

"Never mind... I've provided for you both, haven't I? Treated Tamara like my own. You've never wanted for anything, have you?" Ryan sat down beside her and ran his hands through his hair then rubbed his knuckles. He stared at her, breathing deeply, then reached out to stroke her cheek. Celeste pulled back and covered her swelling eye with her hand. "I'm sorry about that... I lost control. I promise it won't happen again, okay? Now go put some ice on that and get yourself cleaned up. I'll go out and pick up some Arabic mezze down the road. You like that, don't you? You know, hummus, tabbouleh, fattoush... that type of thing. Don't want to eat too heavy, it's getting late."

He patted her knee like nothing had happened and strolled across the foyer towards the door. "And, it's probably not a good idea to tell your friend what just happened, right? We don't want to air our dirty laundry." He turned around and was out the door before Celeste could utter a word.

Dazed and still horrified, Celeste slowly stood up from the couch and headed into the kitchen to get some ice. She wrapped it in a dishtowel, held it to her face and walked quietly into her bedroom and closed the door behind her. She let out a whimper and leaned her face into the cold cloth. She knew she couldn't anger Ryan any further but she also knew she couldn't stay with him any longer. She had known for a long while their marriage was over but couldn't bring herself to leave. He had just made it easier. She would have to put up a good front though until she and Susan were safely back in Dubai. They couldn't leave Saudi without Ryan's approval. He could conceivably keep them here against their will. If he suspected she was thinking of leaving, he would probably send Susan back and keep her there indefinitely... and then what would happen to Tamara? She should feel relief that he had spoken with Tamara, but she still felt unsettled and the feeling would remain until she could talk to Tamara herself. Ryan's story just didn't seem right.

She had to pretend everything was fine. Just until she could convince Ryan she was fully recovered, everything was fine between them and she should go back and get the house set up. *Oh Shit! The house.* How long would the moving company store their belongings? She had to remember to ask... her life was in that container.

Celeste opened her suitcase and pulled out her cosmetic bag. She walked into the bathroom, switched on the light and looked at her eye. It was already turning black and blue but the ice had brought the swelling down. She pulled some concealer out of her bag and gently dabbed some on. The bruise faded slightly under the liquid beige veil but it was impossible to hide it completely. She would have to come up with a plausible story so Susan didn't ask too many questions. She zipped the bag shut, switched off the light and quickly changed into her comfy yoga pants and tank top.

She wandered into the living room and sat down at the piano and began playing her favorite piece. Beethoven's Moonlight Sonata always made her feel better. She hadn't played in a while and missed a few notes but her fingers started to loosen up after the first few bars and she closed her eyes, allowing the music to flow over her like a mother's caressing hands, calming her nerves. Many found the haunting melody a bit sad, but Celeste had always found it uplifting... almost like the composer had looked into her life and knew the tumultuous nature of the beast and how to tame it, sympathetically, with nurturing strokes of musical genius. She had sold her piano when they left Nigeria and she desperately missed playing. She made a promise to herself, then and there, she would buy another... she couldn't believe she had let Ryan talk her into selling it, although moving pianos is a very expensive proposition. She could have rented one while they'd lived in Saudi though. She never should have denied herself this simple pleasure, one that had always helped smooth out her jagged moods.

"Celeste, how beautiful... I didn't know you played." Susan walked into the living room and sat down on the couch.

"Thank you, it helps to relax me," Celeste continued playing, with her back towards Susan.

"This is perfect!" Susan sunk into the soft leather of the couch, leaned back and closed her eyes. "A hot bath with Mick and the boys followed by a serenade of classical music... I think I'm in heaven." She hummed along to the bars that were familiar to her as the music flowed around her like the dance of a hundred veils, caressing her senses. The more she got to know about Celeste, the more she liked her and the more she realized they had in common. Susan's mom played piano too. She had warm memories of her playing Moonlight Sonata, which always took her and her brothers to a happy place... most of the music their mother played had had that effect on them. It could stop a sibling battle from heating up and make them forget what they were fighting over in the first place. It could trigger impromptu sing-alongs or dance parties. Susan's house was always filled with music. If her mother wasn't playing, she was listening to records. She'd stack five at a time on the turntable and the phonograph's arm would automatically drop down the next after one had finished playing. Her mother's taste, from Spike Jone's and the City Slickers and Bing Crosby to Mozart and Beethoven, had helped form Susan's own eclectic music preferences.

As the last note faded, Celeste released the foot pedal, quelling the reverberation. She sat back and put her hands on her lap.

"That was amazing," Susan clapped. "It took me right back to my childhood when my mom used to play for us.

"I'm glad you liked it... if you like I'll play some more later," Celeste turned around on the piano bench to face her friend.

"Oh my God! What happened to your eye?" Susan got up from the couch, covered the distance between them in two big strides and sat next to Celeste on the bench. She put her hand around her shoulder.

"Oh, it's nothing... I went into the bedroom and didn't turn on the light. Walked right into the

bathroom door... silly me." She put her hand on her face then patted Susan's hand on her shoulder.
"Please don't worry, it'll be fine." She got up and motioned to the piano. "Do you play?"

"Oh heavens no," Susan laughed. "I played the ukelele when I was a kid and I can play chopsticks but that's it. I'm more of a music appreciator." She turned sideways and plunked out the first few notes to demonstrate. "Are you sure you're okay?"

"Of course," Celeste walked to the couch and straightened the already plumped and positioned sofa cushions. "Ryan's on his way and will pick up some dinner around the corner... should be back any minute. I'll just get some plates and things." She smiled at Susan and winced as the pressure of her forced grin pushed on her cheekbone.

"Jeez, that looks painful," Susan shook her head. "Did you put some ice on it?" She followed Celeste into the kitchen.

"Yes, it took some of the swelling down... but please don't worry about it. I'll be fine. I'm more embarrassed than anything else." Celeste pulled plates from the cupboard and handed them to Susan. "We've been invited to a wedding this weekend... should be interesting for you... have you ever been to an Arab wedding?"

"No, actually I haven't," Susan walked back into the dining room and spread the plates on the table. She turned and leaned her elbows on the pass-through and took the utensils Celeste held out to her. "We don't really run in those circles," she sighed. "I would love to get an inside look at the culture but the Emiratis are very private people and stick pretty close to their families. Even though Mitch does have Emirati co-workers, they don't really seem to mix with us Westerners for the most part... although of course there are always exceptions to the rule."

"Well, it'll be different from the wedding's you're used to then," Celeste handed her some napkins. "There are actually two receptions... one for the men and one for the women. The only men allowed in the women's party are the groom and a few of his family members... and that only happens at the end of the wedding when the bride and groom sit together like they're on display and everyone offers their best wishes for a happy life. Sometimes the parties are even held on different days in different locations, but it appears for this one the parties are on the same day at the same place."

"That sounds terrific, but I didn't bring anything fancy to wear," Susan poured water from the pitcher that was on the bar trolley.

"I know, I didn't either but Ryan suggested we take his driver and go shopping tomorrow. We need groceries anyway so we can make a day of it."

"Sounds great... I thought maybe our priority would be to start putting together a plan to look for Tamara?" Susan wanted to tread lightly as she knew Celeste was still very fragile. What mother wouldn't be with a child missing? Being busy was crucial.

"Oh... um, actually Ryan said he spoke with her," Celeste's laugh came out more like a squeak. "She's fine and just staying with some friends in Dubai for a while. That's probably why she didn't show up on any passenger lists. Mitch's friend must have seen the wrong name or something," she shrugged.

"You're kidding? Did you talk to her? Does she realize how crazy with worry you've been?" Susan bit her tongue realizing her insensitive use of the word 'crazy'. "I'm sorry... I mean... surely she knew she was causing a lot of trouble by disappearing like that. No phone call, no nothing. I know teenagers can be difficult but that's just cruel." Susan stood with her hands on her hips in disbelief.

"No, I haven't talked with her yet," Celeste's voice caught in her throat and tears welled up in her eyes. "I'm just so relieved she's ok. I'll call her later. I think she lost her cell phone so I have to get her friend's number..."

Susan reached out and gathered Celeste into a big hug. "Thank God she's ok," she tightened her arms around Celeste and felt her heart beating against her own chest.

Celeste pulled away and wiped the tears rolling down her cheeks as Ryan's key turned in the lock. "I'll just go wash my face. Can you please help Ryan put the food out?" Celeste disappeared quickly down the hallway.

"Sure, okay..." Susan knew something was not quite right and could see Celeste was barely hanging on to her last dangling, shredded nerve. She'd seen this so many times in her patients before as they recovered from a bout of depression and knew she'd have to watch her very closely because it could go either way – stumbling back into a pit of deep despair or vaulted into the euphoric state of a manic episode. Neither one was desirable... hopefully she could guide Celeste to land firmly somewhere in the middle. She had a gnawing feeling in her gut that they weren't getting the full story about Tamara and she needed Celeste to be clearheaded.

She turned as Ryan came into the foyer. "Hi Ryan, nice to see you again."

"Hey Susan... great to see you too. I hope you had a comfortable flight. Did they treat you well?" He juggled his keys and the take-away bags and pushed the door closed with his foot.

"Oh yes, it was lovely. Thanks for taking care of that... Here, let me help you with those," she reached for the bags. "The table's set so I'll just get some serving spoons and we'll be good to go... Celeste's washing up."

"Okay, fine... I'll go check on her then," he brushed past her. "Feel free to open a bottle of wine... there's one chilling in the fridge."

"Will do... hey, good news about Tamara... Celeste told me she's been staying with a friend," Susan started.

Ryan was halfway down the hall and called back over his shoulder, "Yes, quite a relief for sure… we'll be right out…" Susan heard his voice cut off as he closed the bedroom door behind him.

## *Chapter 25*

The girls entered the house giggling and talking, loaded down with a mountain of parcels filled with dresses, shoes and even jewelry, all bought for the upcoming wedding celebrations. The theme for the women's party was 'The Great Gatsby', which had been re-popularized with the release of the movie with Leonardo DeCaprio, so they went all out with flapper dresses, feather headbands and long strings of beads, which Aliya insisted be real pearls. She had told Tamara that many younger girls were mixing elements of the traditional Arab wedding with more modern fare like picking a fun theme, often music or movie related. The wedding party was planned for the following night but this night they would be attending the bridal henna party, which was normally reserved for the bride's family. Because Aliya was married to the bride's cousin, she was family by marriage and Tamara would be welcomed as Aliya's houseguest.

Aliya stopped short as she landed on the last of the three stairs that lead into the foyer and Tamara bumped into her. "Hey!" Tamara began and then saw Aliya's father-in-law, Mohammed, standing at the opposite end of the entry, arms crossed and jaw clenched.

"Aliya, please escort our *guest* to her room and then come back and join the family in the *majlis*." He turned on his heel not waiting for her to reply and disappeared into the largest room in the house most often used for mixed family gatherings. Most Arab homes had two (or more) 'living rooms'... one for the men and one for the women.

"He doesn't look happy," Tamara began. "I hope it's nothing we've done."

"I'm sure it isn't," Aliya handed the parcels to the maid who stood quietly nearby and nervously fussed with her headscarf. "Sasha, can you please take these to my rooms and we'll sort them out later, thank-you." The maid nodded and scurried up the stairs. "Come on Tamara, I'd better get you to your room. My father-in-law is not the most patient of men," she whispered and gently took Tamara's elbow.

"Okay... I'll just take a shower then and get ready for tonight... do you think we'll still be going to the henna party?" The girls walked side-by-side up the wide, arching staircase. The deep red carpeting and ornately carved banisters reminded Tamara of the staircase at Tara, Scarlett's mansion in Gone with the Wind, which was her mother's all-time favorite movie.

"Oh I'm sure we will... I can't imagine anything that would stop us from going."

Tamara was relieved as she swallowed the lump unexpectedly rising in her throat at the thought of her mother. She had to admit, she missed her but not the nagging and emotional upheaval. She was actually enjoying this little break from her family drama. It was good to see that other families, no matter how rich and well connected they were, had conflicts too. Sometimes being a third culture kid, not living in either parent's home country and being born elsewhere, was really cool. Other times it sucked... like when people asked you where you were from. Tamara still didn't quite know how to answer that. Her parents were American; she was born in Nigeria and lived in the Middle East. She knew she was lucky and the vast majority of her peers in the Western world would never have the opportunities she had. She was excited about seeing what an Arab bachelorette party and wedding was like... but being 'escorted' back to her room was a harsh reminder that she really was a prisoner of sorts. She prayed her father would sort out whatever shit he was going through and come for her soon... *but not before the wedding,* she thought.

Aliya slipped into the *majlis* and sat on the cushion next to her husband. Her father-in-law, Mohammed, conferred in the far corner with a tall man who wore a black, silky *bicht* with gold trim over his long, white *dishdasha*. She wondered why this gentleman was wearing the traditional Arab formal dress.

"Who is the man with your father," she whispered to Yusef.

Their angry whispers were punctuated by Mohammed's wildly flailing arms.

"That's Bashir, the Minister of Commerce and Industry," he leaned over and explained quietly. "Khalid's father."

"I didn't recognize him... he doesn't look at all like his picture. What's he doing here?" The Minister was a cousin of Yusef and his father and Aliya did know the Minister's son, Khalid, but had not met the Minister in person. She pulled her veil tighter over the bottom half of her face and secured it under her headscarf. Even though the Minister was technically family she was shy and felt the need to be fully covered in his presence. She cringed as he turned to study her with piercing brown eyes, as dark as the crude oil that bubbled up from the desert sand. Even though it was hot in the *majlis*, she shivered and moved closer to her husband, yet still keeping a 'polite' distance. Public displays of affection were not allowed and, even for married couples, must wait until they were behind closed doors.

"We've had some bad news..." Yusef whispered and shook his head slowly. "Ali..." he paused and turned to her bewildered. She saw tears spring from the gentle eyes she had fallen in love with and her heart skipped a beat. He leaned closer and said quietly, "Ali is dead."

"What? No... it can't be. What happened?"

"They're trying to figure that out.... It was either suicide or..." his voice cracked.

"Or what?"

Yusef stared into his coffee cup and swirled a sugar stick round and round, without looking up.

"Or what? Yusef, tell me." Aliya took the cup from Yusef's hands. Ali had meant so much to him. They had practically grown up together. Ali's family had worked for Yusef's family for three generations.

"Or murder." He ran the back of his hand roughly across his eyes and down the side of his face, obliterating the tears that had unexpectedly escaped.

Aliya gasped and without thinking threw her arms around her husband to console him. He stiffened and she quickly realized what she was doing and looked towards her father-in-law and his visitor as her hands fell to her lap. They were deep in an intense conversation and hadn't noticed. She leaned back in a daze.

"Drink some tea my dear," Ranya, Mohammed's number one wife and Yusef's mother handed her the sugary mix. Aliya hadn't even heard her come in and sit beside them.

"I can't believe this... it's so hard to fathom," Aliya took the cup offered. "Has anyone told Fahad?"

"No, we haven't," said Yusef. "He's out picking up the henna you need for the ladies party tonight."

"Well, call him and tell him to come home! I don't think we should be going to a party tonight. I'll tell Tamara we won't be going." Aliya got up to leave.

"No, you won't," Yusef reached for her hand and pulled her back down beside him. "We can't let this put a damper on the wedding. It wouldn't be fair to the bride and groom. They didn't know Ali and wouldn't understand our sorrow." He glanced towards his father who was finally escorting the Minister out to the foyer. "Besides, there will be more than 100 women there tonight who have heard of 'Aliya the Artist' and will be anxiously waiting for you to apply a piece of art on their hands."

"I wish I hadn't offered," sighed Aliya. "I shouldn't leave the family while there's such turmoil."

"Don't worry about it. We'll be fine... and besides, she has no sisters and you're married to her eldest male cousin so you must go..." Yusef's words were cut off as Mohammed stormed back into the *majlis* and began pacing in the center of the room, back and forth in front of his family.

"Yusef, call Mr. Parker at his office and get him here at once. Enough of this *diplomacy*. If we find out he had anything to do with Ali's death, I want him to know that he will also be responsible for his own daughter's death, maybe not by his own hand, but by his actions!"

"Father, why not wait and see if you can speak with him at the wedding tomorrow?" Yusef began tentatively. "And, perhaps it would be better to wait and see what the Minister wants to do."

Mohammad grunted and continued his pacing and ranting, while Aliya, Yusef and Ranya quietly watched. Ranya gripped Aliya's hand. They both knew his wrath could escalate, especially under these circumstances. Aliya wished she could do something to calm him down but also knew not to interrupt him during a tirade. She felt sick to her stomach and her mind was racing. Was Mohammed referring to Tamara? What could Tamara's father have to do with this? She had grown quite fond of their houseguest and hadn't thought about or asked many questions about why she was staying with them as Tamara was a welcome diversion. Aliya didn't have many friends and the only women she spent time with usually were Yusef's mother, his father's other two wives and a few female cousins. She needed to find out more and would question her husband further and have him assure her that no harm would come to Tamara.

"Aliya," Mohammed growled and she started. "Go to your friend and get yourselves ready for the bride's gathering. Make sure you tell no one what you've seen or heard. Nothing... you understand."

# Chapter 26

Tamara chatted excitedly about the evening ahead as Aliya stared out the window of the limo, twisting the handles of the bag on her lap that held all of her *rani kona*, multiple tubes filled with her henna paste. She knew there was more to Ali's death than Yusef would admit and her gut told her it had something to do with Tamara. She tried to recall the conversation with her father-in-law when he told her they were going to have a houseguest and needed her to help. She remembered at one point, Yusef telling her that Tamara's father worked for the Ministry but he didn't give any details. Initially, she questioned why Tamara's door had to be locked from the outside but all Mohammed would tell her was that it was for her own good. When she pushed Yusef for an answer, he repeated the same thing and simply added that it was his father's wish. She didn't want to be disrespectful so left it at that but so many other questions rolled around in her head, refusing to let up, giving rise to more. Mohammed's anger from this afternoon seemed to have dissipated but Aliya knew it could erupt again at any time and was afraid for Tamara's life. She hadn't quite put the pieces together but she would.

"Aliya, you're a million miles away! Did you hear what I asked?"

"I'm so sorry Tamara..." Aliya turned towards her trying to think quickly of an excuse to explain why she was so distracted. "I'm a little nervous about being the *Henaya* tonight," she said. "It's such an honor and so important, I hope I don't disappoint her."

"Don't worry. The designs you showed me are gorgeous," Tamara put her hand on Aliya's and squeezed it. "I know you're going to be awesome. So, how many girls do you think will be there tonight?"

"Oh, I'm not really sure... but since the family is so closely connected, there will most likely be at least a hundred or more, I would guess."

"Do you mean like 'connected'," Tamara made quote marks in the air with her fingers, "such as to the royal family?" She giggled and rolled her eyes. "Am I going to meet a bunch of *real* princesses?"

"I am sure you will," Aliya smiled at Tamara's lightly veiled sarcasm. They both knew that in Saudi, there were so many 'princes' and 'princesses' you were bound to run into a few no matter where you went. "But, these ones will be close relatives of the King since the Minister is a first cousin. Their mothers were sisters. The ladies at the party tonight will most likely be first cousins, nieces or granddaughters."

"I'll be sure to mind my manners," Tamara smiled back.

Aliya peered into her bag again. "I hope I brought enough... it wouldn't do to run out."

"I guess this is it..." Tamara pointed out the window as they pulled up to a mansion surrounded by an eight-foot marble wall. Their driver pulled up to a huge double, wrought iron gate with shiny yellow metallic globes perched on top of each of two obelisks flanking the entrance. "Is that real gold?" Tamara wondered as the gate swung open silently on its hydraulic hinges.

"I'm sure it is," Aliya offered. "And, this is the right place... see the huge banner hanging from the roof?"

"Yeah."

"That shows the wedding date, which is tomorrow, in Arabic scroll. It's tradition to have one hanging over the door of the bride's home."

"That's weird," Tamara fiddled with her headscarf, tucking in a blond strand that had escaped. Her hair was so fine, like wisps of raw silk that it kept sliding out. "But I guess you do that instead of an announcement in the newspaper."

"Hmmm..." Aliya was busy gathering her bags and giving instructions to the driver to retrieve the gifts from the trunk for the bride and the bride's mother from Yusef's mother and Mohammed's other wives. They had decided not to join the party so they could be home when the news of Ali's death was shared with his brother. Aliya was to make their apologies and say they would be at the wedding the next day.

The girls entered the foyer and were escorted to the ladies' salon where the decibel level of excited chatter was almost deafening. The room was filled with a hundred dark haired beauties, wearing the latest fashions off the Paris and New York runways. As soon as the door had closed behind them, off came their *abayas*, *shaylas* and in some cases *burquas*, often worn by women of the older generation, which covered the entire face with a mesh or other thin fabric panel to look through. In the safe, man-free zone, these Saudi women strutted around in form-fitting, revealing gowns, teetering on the highest heels, many with the telltale red soles of French designer Christian Louboutin. Precious gems sparkled like searchlights from ears, necks and fingers and false eyelashes circled big brown eyes, lined with dark kohl and topped with bright blue, purple and rose eye shadow.

Aliya and Tamara were ushered into a cloakroom where they removed their outer attire. The female attendant carefully hung each of their *abayas* on a silk-covered hanger and handed them the corresponding numbers for later retrieval.

"Aliya, there you are! How lovely to see you."

Aliya turned around as a statuesque woman floated towards her with pure elegance. "Hello Marta," the women clasped hands and kissed each other on both cheeks twice. "I'd like to introduce you to my friend Tamara who is staying with us. Tamara, this is Marta, the mother of the bride."

"It's such a pleasure to meet you," Tamara almost curtsied. "Thank you so much for inviting me."

"You are most welcome in my home," Marta said graciously and took Tamara's hands in hers and leaned in to kiss both cheeks. She dropped one of Tamara's hands and turned towards Aliya. "Now, let us go and see the bride. She's been waiting for you to do her henna. Come!" She led Tamara through the sprawling room by the hand towards the bride seated at the front on a pedestal, like she was on display. A hush fell on the crowd and the music stopped as everyone stared at the blonde stranger being escorted by the mother of the bride, which was a great honor.

While Aliya did her duty, Tamara cruised the sweets table... mini-tarts filled with dates and the Baklava that she loved with the flaky phylo dough covered with crushed pistachio nuts were surrounded by fresh fruit, whole dates and a variety of nuts. She took in the selection of almond-filled dates, chocolate covered dates and dates rolled in icing sugar. Tamara didn't really get the Arab love affair with dates but remembered her friends in Dubai talking excitedly about the Liwa Date Festival, which she thought was equally as ridiculous as the camel beauty contest. She thought they had to be the ugliest animals on the planet but the contest winners were bought and sold for millions. She sighed and popped a chocolate covered date in her mouth...the only way she would eat one.

As she wandered from table to table, sampling the *Lailet al Hinna* (Night of Henna) feast, she noticed the other girls whispering and pointing at her. It didn't really bother her as she was always the 'odd' one in any room. In Nigeria, she was often the only white girl, except when she finally started kindergarten and went to the international school meant for foreign service workers' kids but somehow her dad managed to get her in. Of course, the years they lived in Saudi, she was the rare blond-haired, blue-eyed girl, with no one else like her for miles, other than her mother.

A young girl about 10 years old with big brown eyes lined with kohl reached up and touched the ends of Tamara's hair and looked at her in wonder. "*Amrekeea?*" she asked shyly backing away as Tamara turned.

Tamara smiled at her. "Um, actually... well, ah, sort of... I was born in Nigeria but I have an American passport since my parents are American..." her words trailed off as she realized by the girl's puzzled look that she didn't speak English. Tamara nodded. The girl covered her mouth and laughing, ran off to her circle of friends nearby, tittering about her 'encounter' with the '*Amrekeea*', the American woman.

"Don't mind them," Aliya had come up beside her and took her by the arm. "They're just silly little girls who rarely meet anyone who isn't just like them."

"Oh, it's okay," Tamara shrugged. "They're adorable carrying their little Louis Vuitton jeweled clutch purses. I wonder what they carry in them?"

"Probably a lip gloss and some Juicy fruit gum," Aliya laughed. "Come... I've finished the bride's henna. Come and see, and then I'll do yours."

## *Chapter 27*

As they turned from Mekkah Road onto the long winding driveway heading towards the entrance to the Ritz Carleton, Susan watched out the window in awe. They were one of an extended line of luxury cars and stretch limos, inching along, moving through three different security check points, showing ID and invitations, ultimately to spill their royal cargo into the grand entrance of the opulent five-star resort.

Susan, Celeste and Ryan rode in the back of one of the company's Lincoln SUVs with soft tan leather, a built in bar and flat screen TV. Susan had experienced a lot of luxury living lately. As the wife of an Emirates pilot she was able to fly first class. It was so easy to take for granted but she knew she shouldn't get used to it. Once Mitch was no longer with the airline, they would both be back in economy class... but she would enjoy it while it lasted. The people in the stretch Rolls Royces and Bentleys ahead were way out of her league but she would do her best to fit in.

They passed by at least half a mile of lush, landscaped gardens. Susan had read that the hotel sat on 52 acres and imagined the hundreds of colorful blooms and the intoxicating fragrances that must infuse every corner of the grounds. She also wondered how much the utility bill was to keep it all watered and green.

"This is so exciting... I've never seen anything like it," Susan pulled the zipper of her *abaya* up to the top.

"Make sure your hair is covered too when we go in," Ryan reminded them both. "My bosses will be there and we want to make sure you make a good impression." He eyed them up and down.

"Of course... don't forget, we did live here together for a few years. I know how to behave," Celeste fastened her *abaya*, re-positioned her headscarf and pushed in her hair.

"Sometimes you need to be reminded," he said as he tucked her scarf more closely around her neck to make sure no skin was showing at all. "So, when we go in, there's a brief reception in the foyer. I'm told the entire hotel is booked for the wedding. After I introduce you to a few people and we make some polite conversation, we'll split and go to different parties, one for the bride and the women and one for the groom and the men. I'll introduce you to Miriam, the Minister's executive assistant and Sheri, my old assistant who now also works in the Minister's office on special projects. You'll go with them."

"Oh that'll be helpful to go in with someone who knows the drill," Susan attempted to lighten the mood. Ryan seemed wound up as tight as a drum and Celeste sat stiffly next to him, not touching, checking her teeth in a compact mirror, probably to make sure there was no lipstick on them. Susan wondered again what had really happened back at the apartment. She stole a glance at Celeste who had managed to cover up most of the bruise under her eye with some carefully applied cover up and a thick layer of foundation and some creative placement of brightly colored eye shadows. Fortunately, it was typical for Arab women to wear heavy eye make-up so Celeste would fit right in. She actually had flair for make-up application, and looked stunning. Susan had opted for more subtle eye shadows but still felt elegant in the sapphire blue designer dress by Valentino that Celeste had helped pick out. It was ridiculously expensive but Ryan had insisted on paying, claiming that he could use it as a 'business expense.'

Their driver pulled up and a tall, regal-looking gentleman with skin as dark as mahogany reached over to open the door for them.

"He looks like a Masai warrior," Susan whispered to Celeste as they got out.

"He may well be," Celeste agreed as she nodded her thanks to the seven-foot valet who bowed in reply.

Celeste pulled gently on Susan's arm as she started to walk towards the entrance and held her back until Ryan came around from the other side to join them. They then followed two-paces behind him as all of the other black-clad women were demonstrating. Susan raised her eyebrows at Celeste who shrugged and pursed her lips.

"It's too bad Tamara's not with us," Celeste said. "She would have really enjoyed the experience."

"For Christ's sake Celeste, she's busy with her friends," Ryan turned around and hissed. "Now, no more talk about her, okay?"

"Alright, fine... I just miss her," Celeste stood firm. "When we get back to the apartment I'm going to email her and tell her. At least she'll know she's missed, even if she doesn't want to talk to me. Maybe if I send a message on Facebook she'll get it... she's constantly checking that. I can't believe I didn't think of that before."

"I'm sure she'd love to hear from you," Susan linked her arm through Celeste's. "Tell her we'll have a girl's day at the spa when we get back. I think we all deserve a little pampering."

"Do what you want," Ryan waved his hand dismissing the idea.

They entered the magnificent foyer of the hotel, complete with four life-sized bronze stallions reared up on pedestals in each of the four corners. Susan tried to keep her mouth closed so she didn't look like a poor relation from the country. A white-gloved waiter approached and offered a silver tray piled with Arabic Mezze. She took the cocktail napkin offered and chose a stuffed grape leaf and a *kibbe*. She bit into the oblong, fried croquette filled with onion and minced lamb and enjoyed the savory taste sensation. The waiter offered the tray to Celeste and Ryan.

"Ah, no, thank-you..." he waved the waiter away. "Here comes Karl..."

"Ryan, I'm glad you could make it," Karl shook hands with Ryan. He turned to the women, bowed and put his hand over his heart, the customary greeting between men and women in Saudi. "*As-Salaam-Alaikum*, Celeste. It's been a long time."

"*Wa Alaikum-As-Salaam*," replied Celeste. "Yes, I think the last time I saw you was in Cambridge a hundred years ago at graduation." Celeste turned to Susan. "Susan, this is Khalid... or Karl. Ryan, Karl and Donald, my late husband, were all roommates in college. Karl, this is my good friend, Susan. We know each other from Dubai."

"So lovely to meet you," Susan put her hand to her heart. She couldn't help noticing the slight blush that had heightened the already pink color on Celeste's cheeks and the wide grin on the devastatingly handsome Karl.

"And you," Karl smiled warmly and turned to Celeste. "I hope you're feeling better. Ryan tells me you've been ill?"

"Oh, I'm much better, thank you for asking."

"I'm glad to hear it. You look well and, quite honestly, you haven't changed one bit... just as beautiful as ever."

"When did you become such a charmer Karl?" Ryan stepped in front of Celeste. "You've spent so much time in the U.S. you've forgotten that it's not appropriate to flirt with a man's wife... especially here, even if you are the boss."

"I wasn't flirting, just stating the obvious," Karl winked at Celeste, and Susan could see Ryan's shoulder's tense.

"Yeah, right... okay, we've got to find Miriam and Sheri," Ryan corralled the women with his arm, ushering them away from Karl. "I'll meet you in the men's party then, alright?"

"Sure... let's all have dinner some time and catch up properly," Karl directed his comment to Celeste, then turned to Susan. "It was a pleasure to meet you, Susan. Enjoy your visit."

"Thank-you... *Shukran*..." Before Susan could finish her reply, Ryan's hand was on her back pushing her towards the signs for 'Ballroom B, Bride's Party'.

"There's Miriam... hurry up!" Ryan continued to guide them. "You don't want to keep the bride waiting."

"Ryan, stop pushing, I'm going to trip over my *abaya*," Celeste side-stepped just out of his reach and paused to adjust the shoulders of her cloak that had gone askew. "With this crowd, I'm sure the bride won't know whether we're there or not."

As they approached Miriam, Susan noticed a petite young woman standing next to her. Even cloaked in the ubiquitous *abaya* her tiny frame was obvious. She had the biggest hazel eyes Susan had ever seen. The long false eyelashes certainly emphasized their size but Susan was sure that even without make-up, she was a knockout.

"Hello Miriam... Sheri," Ryan poured on the charm. "Miriam, this is my wife, Celeste and her friend Susan." He stepped aside to allow the ladies to acknowledge one another. "Celeste, you know Sheri. She worked for Rydo in Lagos with us. She's just accepted a very prestigious position in the Minister's office. We're very proud of her."

"Yes... so nice to see you again," Celeste smiled and bowed her head. "Ryan was so pleased you were able to join him here to help with the Kingdom Center Project. Congratulations on your new job... I'm sure Ryan's going to miss you."

"She'll still be doing special projects for the Minister so I'm sure our paths will cross frequently." He smiled a smile that made Susan's skin prickle. *Was there something going on between them?*

"Shall we go in ladies?" Miriam took control and nodded at Ryan. "I'm sure you're all eager to join the celebrations."

"Of course," Ryan tipped his head slightly, deferring to Miriam. "Celeste, let's say we meet back here by 11. That should give us all enough time to enjoy the festivities and give our regards to the bride and groom and not tire you too much... you are still recovering."

"That's fine. We'll see you then," Celeste agreed, hooked her arm into the crook of Susan's and turned to follow Miriam and Sheri into the ballroom.

Ryan wound his way through the crowded foyer and down the hall, following the signs to 'Ballroom A – Groom's Party'. As far as he was concerned the evening couldn't be over soon enough. His mind was reeling trying to work out a plan to extricate himself from his tenuous situation. He scanned the room and wondered why he was even still alive. They couldn't have discovered the extent of his embezzlement. He could still shift the blame to Ali if he played his cards right, couldn't he? Or, was it just a matter of time until they uncovered the depth of his deceit? He had to create an escape plan. He would hire a small plane discreetly to fly him out... maybe to Africa. He could be out of Saudi airspace before they even knew he'd gone and, if he chose his location carefully, he could make sure they would never find him.

His heart gave a twinge as he realized he couldn't leave without knowing Tamara was safe. Even though she wasn't his biological daughter, he had still raised her as his own and loved her very much.

She was so smart and funny. She always managed to bring a smile to his face even during the most stressful times. Life had been tough in Lagos but, when she was a child, as long as she had a butterfly to chase or a flower to pick, her youthful giggles filled the air and made everything joyful. As a teenager she was a little less carefree but they still shared a strong bond. He mentally shook himself. *Don't let your emotions get the best of you Parker. It's a weakness you can't afford right now.*

Taking in his surroundings brought him back to the present. He admired the opulence of the ballroom, from the gargantuan crystal chandelier hanging in the center of the ceiling to the gold encrusted candelabras that adorned each of the round banquet tables filling the room. He thought about how much money was wasted at these wedding parties. He knew that this type of party would cost at least a couple million; each ballroom could accommodate about 1,400 people and there was obviously no expense spared. The room was packed and Ryan assumed the women's party would be full to capacity as well.

There was a group of musicians, a traditional Arab ensemble or *takht,* on a raised platform off to one side. Their music was amplified to a decibel high enough to make Ryan's ear drums vibrate. The younger men gathered in a large open area to demonstrate their prowess at traditional Arab dance, each one holding what looked like a cane; they tapped the floor in rhythmic syncopation and swayed to the music, following the same steps in unison like a Western line-dance minus the 'boot scootin' and belt buckles. The 'dance floor' took up at least two thirds of the ballroom.

"I know what you did to Ali," Mohammed had come up silently from behind and hissed in Ryan's ear. "You will pay for it and so will your family."

"I don't know what you're talking about," Ryan calmly turned to face the old man whose steely glare was like staring into the eyes of a demon. He looked familiar but Ryan couldn't quite place him. "And, who exactly are you? I don't believe we've met.

"I am Mohammed, cousin of Bashir," he stepped back and eyed Ryan from head to toe like he was measuring him for a coffin or a shallow grave. "Ali, your foreman, was like family. His family has worked for mine for generations."

"What do you mean 'was'," Ryan raised his eyebrows feigning surprise. His mind searched quickly for an appropriate response. "The last I saw him, he was a little agitated but seemed fine... the grand opening of the Kingdom Center is coming up and he was stressed that we wouldn't make the deadline. I assured him it would be fine." He raised his voice to be heard above the music and cane clacking.

"You know what has happened and you are responsible," Mohammed leaned close. "You had better sleep with one eye open and pray for your lovely daughter as well... I feel your actions will have grave results." He fired another piercing glare in Ryan's direction.

"What do you know about my daughter?" Ryan's voice raised another octave.

"Ah... your daughter... she's closer than you think."

"If you harm a hair on her head..." his comment was lost in the cacophony of drums as Mohammed turned on his heel and promptly got lost in the crowd of swirling white robes.

"Shit!" Ryan's control of the situation was rapidly slipping away and a knot the size of a fist tightened in the pit of his stomach. Tamara was his... he had raised her as his own and he would do everything he could to make sure these bastards couldn't have her.

# Chapter 28

As soon as they walked into the room the combined aroma of cardamom from the Arabic coffee and *oud,* the powerful, woody scented perfume popular with the ladies of the Middle East, swirled around Tamara, making her a little light-headed. They had been escorted through a VIP entrance and came out at the front of the room just a few feet from where the bride perched on her pedestal. Tamara admired the intricate work that Aliya had done on the bride's hands. She could see part of the lace pattern on the top of her feet and toes that poked out of her blue suede sandals, selected to match the blue and gold traditional Bedouin gown the bride had chosen, rather than the Western-influenced white gowns Arab bride's often chose these days. She recalled a similar pattern from the past... the intricate design on the lace curtains they had in their kitchen in Nigeria. She smiled at the memory.

The bride's guests had taken 'The Great Gatsby' theme to heart. Many of the ladies, including Tamara herself, strolled the ballroom, clad from head to toe in flamboyant flapper dresses with strings of pearls and elaborate feathered and jeweled head pieces that Tamara was sure would rival any of the attendees' of the fictitiously famed Gatsby parties.

The ballroom overflowed with exuberance coming from each sub-themed corner. Shrieks of laughter came from the Charleston dance section where a demonstration and lessons were underway. The far side of the room sported a full-sized trapeze with tightrope walker, jugglers and airborne acrobatics that reminded Tamara of the show she had seen as a kid at Phuket Fantasy in Thailand... only more elaborate, and minus the elephants... none that she saw yet anyway. Beyond that were belly dancers and pole dancers sporadically positioned throughout the room. Silver and gold streamers flowed from the ceiling forming shimmering partitions, providing semi-private seating areas for smaller groups.

"It's absolutely crazy," Tamara grabbed Aliya's hand and squeezed it. "I'm so glad we could come."

"I am too," Aliya squeezed back. "We can't stay long though so let's go see what there is to eat."

"Ha... more like, what isn't there to eat?" Tamara laughed and her eyes scanned the buffet tables that flanked the ballroom on both sides overflowing with food and drink as far as the eye could see.

Celeste scanned the sweets table and absently popped a chocolate covered date into her mouth. She inhaled the soothing steam coming off her Jasmine tea and took in her surroundings. They were at the very back of the room but could still see the bride, who sat up high on a platform to be admired by all her guests... 1,500 of her *closest* friends Celeste calculated, taking in the overflowing ballroom. The bride re-arranged the flowing folds of the rich turquoise satin and Celeste caught a flash of red on the sole of the shoe. *Christian Louboutins... what else would you expect?* The platform slowly rotated so everyone had a three-dimensional, wrap around view to appreciate the full effect of the intricate embroidery of the gown.

"I wonder how she does that," Susan's question broke into her thoughts.

"Does what?"

"That..." Susan pointed to a belly dancer that shimmied her hips close by.

"Years of practice... and no babies," Celeste patted her belly and gave her very best fake pout.

"Do you think the bride's gown is an original... it's spectacular even from way back here," Susan noted.

"Hmmm... I'm sure it is. Did you notice the *Louboutins*?"

"Of course... they're hard to miss, although you've got to look between these gaudy streamers." Susan waved her hand towards the offending shimmering curtain that hung from the ceiling every 20 or 30 feet. The closest one partially separated the buffet table from a nearby circus platform. Each flutter of the silvery strands exposed a glimpse of a contortionist posing as a pretzel.

"The gown was designed by Khalid Khalil," Miriam sidled up and entered the conversation. "He designs for all the royal family."

"I think I've even heard of him," Susan laughed. "Miriam, can I ask you, why are there two cushions on the platform? Will we actually get a chance to see the groom?"

"It's possible," Miriam shared as she guided them along the buffet table. "The groom and his family will come much later and he will join his bride on the platform briefly before they head to the marriage bed."

The three leaned their heads in closer together as the volume of the music increased and the room erupted into a high pitched tongue trill as the older women in the crowd surrounded the bride in ululation.

Celeste gave up trying to hear what Miriam was saying and stepped back to let her finish explaining the intricacies of the Arab wedding traditions to Susan. She couldn't concentrate anyway and didn't feel like being there at all. All she could think of was Tamara. Celeste took another sip of her tea, which by then had gone cold. She set her cup down and watched the undulating crowd, vibrant with the colors of a tropical fish tank. Belly dancers sashayed up to unsuspecting ladies and drew them in with long silky veils. Long strings of beads swung from the necks of at least 200 girls crowding the dance floor, learning to do the Charleston, the fringes on their flapper dresses frantically fluttering. Celeste reached for a glass of mango juice and turned back to watch the festivities. She gasped and the glass slipped from her fingers and crashed to the floor. Her hand flew to her mouth.

"Celeste, what is it? You look as if you've seen a ghost," Susan had to shout to be heard.

"It's Tamara... up there," Celeste pointed to the front of the room.

"I don't see her," Susan soothed. "I've only seen one other blond in the room other than you and it was Sheri... are you sure it wasn't her?"

"No!" Celeste shook Susan's hand from her elbow and started pushing her way through the crowd. "Tamara!" she called, her voice drowned out by a renewed frenzy of ululing. The crowd closed around her, and she caught another glimpse of the blond she initially spied, only this time she saw her face... it was Tamara! She kept pushing trying to keep an eye on her. She broke out of the crowd and ran across the dance floor dodging the swinging arms of the dancers. She pushed aside the curtains of streamers as she went, and in between lost sight of the long, silky mane of hair she was sure was her daughter's. A mother just knows. Celeste stopped and spun around in circles, calling Tamara's name, frantically scanning the crowd, having lost sight of her.

Susan caught up to her, breathless. "Celeste, calm down. Are you sure it was her? It was probably just Sheri... see? They do look alike."

Sheri was walking towards them.

"I know I saw my daughter... she's here," Celeste insisted. She clenched her jaw, determined.

"What about what Ryan said? That she's with a friend in Dubai?" Susan asked.

"I think he's been lying. Something's going on. He's been so on edge lately and I just don't believe him any more. I wanted to... desperately wanted to believe that Tamara's okay but I just know she would have called."

"Well, if she is here, we'll find her," Susan agreed. "But, we have to be sure. It won't help if we create a scene at this wedding."

Sheri came up to them, "Is everything okay? You look upset."

"I just saw... ah..." Celeste stopped as Susan pinched her arm.

"Celeste thought she saw someone she knew and was excited to connect with an old friend," Susan interrupted. "But I guess they've gone to the restroom or something."

"I think we should find Mr. Parker and he can take you home," Sheri began.... "Oh, there's Miriam. I'll let her know you're leaving, okay?"

Susan put her arm around Celeste's shoulder, rubbed the spot she had pinched and guided her towards the exit. "Sorry about that... I believe you," she whispered in her ear. "Let's play it cool and we'll figure it out together."

Tamara had barely had time to finish her plate of assorted mezze that she had carefully selected when a petite blond rushed up to Aliya and whispered something to her. Aliya looked puzzled but nodded and told Tamara they must leave and they were whisked away through the back hallway where they had come in and into the waiting limo.

"It would have been nice to see the groom but at least we had a chance to see the bride in her wedding gown," Tamara had pined, wiping a drip of *hummus* from her chin. *These people are so strange*, she thought to herself as she settled back into the soft leather and wondered who the blond was... the only other blond in the entire room of more than a thousand women. Aliya stared out the window and fidgeted with her sleeves. Tamara suspected something was definitely up her ass. She decided to wait until they got back to the house to ask who the other blond was and what the hell was up.

Ryan was pacing outside the entrance to the hotel taking a deep drag on a cigarette when Susan and Celeste finally came out of the lady's room.

"What the hell's going on Celeste?" He flicked the cigarette onto the drive. "Miriam just had one of the butlers drag me away from a very serious conversation with the Minister's cousin. Do you remember Ali, the foreman on the project?" He didn't wait for her to reply. "Well, he was found dead on the grounds of my office building. It's terribly inconvenient timing... we've still got a lot to do to meet the deadline for the grand opening and..."

"Ryan! Are you listening to yourself?" Celeste stopped him mid-sentence. "That poor man... do they know what happened?"

"I suspect he jumped," Ryan shook his head and shrugged his shoulders. "Celeste, is it really necessary for us to leave? For Christ's sake... do you know how this looks?"

"I thought I saw Tamara but I'm not sure now..." she stopped as Susan threw her a look.

"We're pretty sure it was Sheri... Celeste made a mistake. It's understandable... she misses Tamara terribly. It's not unusual for someone who's been through what Celeste has to imagine things. She'll be fine." She squeezed Celeste around her shoulders.

"I guess I'm just not in the mood for a party. I need to talk to Tamara. Please take me back..." Celeste fought back the urge to scream and pummel Ryan into telling her the truth and for being such an insensitive jerk. But, she knew by the clench of his jaw and the set of his shoulders that there was no reaching him. His cold stare was worse than she'd ever seen before and it sent a jolt like a cattle prod through to the core of her very being. She was glad Susan was there to give her the strength she needed to stand up to him this time.

"Celeste, as usual, you're overreacting... these outbursts are getting tedious," he waved his hand in the general direction of the line-up of limos and the white Lincoln SUV that had delivered them earlier slipped elegantly out of its place in line, drove up and glided to a stop in front of them. "I thought the meds would take care of that."

*Finding my daughter will take care of that you prick!* Celeste's mind screamed. "I think I forgot to take it today..." she replied out loud instead and lowered her eyes so he couldn't see the hate.

"Jesus Susan, I thought that's why we brought you here," Ryan brushed past and took the seat presented as the chauffeur opened the car door. The two women exchanged a look of solidarity and walked to the opposite side and followed suit, nodded their thanks to the chauffeur and slid into the seats behind Ryan.

Ryan plugged in his headset and proceeded to make calls to sub-contractors. Celeste leaned her head back and closed her eyes, happy to be ignored for a while. Her heart was racing and her mind was in a close second. She couldn't wait to be alone with Susan so they could make a plan. She was thinking clearer now than she had in a very long time. She had been led and intimidated by others her whole life. It was time to break free.

## Chapter 29

Aliya closed and locked Tamara's bedroom door behind them. The entire household, other than the servants, was still at the wedding. She didn't want to take the chance of being overheard, as gossip ran rampant among the helpers and flowed unabated into other homes. Story telling was the only real entertainment these people had. Aliya often felt sorry for them but the servants in Mohammed's home were treated better than many others but there was still a division in status and she knew it would be dangerous for them if they became privy to the details behind Tamara's 'visit'.

Aliya had put most of the pieces together from the limited information Yusef had shared, the heated discussions between Mohammed and his recent visitors and the stories Tamara had shared with her about her family. Their urgent departure from the wedding through the back hallways confirmed there were still people who could bring harm to Tamara, but she couldn't figure out whom. Aliya hated the thought her own father-in-law would hurt her but it was even more disturbing to think that it was Tamara's own father. She heard the word 'embezzle' when the Minister was talking to Mohammed, and Aliya assumed it was in reference to Tamara's father. Yusef kept telling her they were protecting Tamara and it was for her own safety that they weren't to tell anyone who Tamara was... only that she was a friend from school. When Aliya asked more questions he became silent. She had a sinking suspicion Tamara was the hammer the Minister was using to torture her father and Aliya didn't like being a part of it.

"It was so great to get out... and what a cool party," Tamara unwound the *shayla* from around her head and tossed it on the bed. "Thanks for taking me Aliya."

"Oh... Um, you're welcome," Aliya lowered herself slowly onto the sofa in the mini-salon across from the bed.

"I wanted to see the groom though. The empty pillow beside the bride was a little sad. I don't understand why they have separate parties."

"It's an old tradition," Aliya explained. "And, it allows the women to uncover and enjoy themselves."

"I guess so... but honestly I don't understand the covering thing either... but I respect your culture and totally get that I have to follow the rules of the country I'm in," Tamara rolled her eyes and plopped down on the bed. "I've been doing that all my life."

"It must be tough to live somewhere where you can't really be who you are," Aliya unzipped her *abaya*. "The Koran tells us we must guard our modesty for greater purity. Isn't that a good thing no matter what your religious beliefs are?"

"I suppose so but I think covering from head to toe is a bit extreme... but I'm just sayin'..." Tamara hopped off the bed and padded over to the closet. "I love this dress and hate to take it off but I'm going to put some comfies on. Can you hang out for a while? I'll be right out." She headed towards the en suite bathroom.

"Yes, I can... actually, I need to talk to you about something important anyway. I'll have Sasha bring some tea."

"Sounds serious," Tamara turned and scowled. "Have you heard from my dad? Is my mom coming? She must be going out of her mind," she sniffed and shook her head. "It doesn't take much to set her off but not keeping tabs on me every single second of the day would be driving her crazy." Tamara sat back down on the bed and faced Aliya. "So, what's up?"

"What about that tea?" Aliya said stalling, not sure how to approach the subject.

"Are you kidding? I'm so full I think I'm gonna burst," Tamara puffed her cheeks out and patted her stomach. "Come on... you look like your best friend died... and, you're scaring me now."

Alyia inhaled and exhaled deeply. "Someone did die..." her voice caught in her throat and tears threatened. She swallowed.

"Oh my God... who? Alyia, what's going on? When can I leave?" Tamara's voice quivered as she glanced towards the locked door.

"Soon... I think... soon," Aliya looked at the key in her hand and quietly slid it into her pocket. "Oh dear, I'm not really handling this very well. I can't think of where to start." She pinched the bridge of her nose, praying for courage and forgiveness for what she was about to do. It would be a betrayal of her husband and father-in-law's trust but she had become fond of Tamara and she didn't deserve to be locked away. She hadn't done anything wrong.

Aliya patted the cushion next to her on the sofa. "Please come... sit with me." Tamara sat down and Aliya reached over, gently taking both her hands and began to tell her everything she knew.

The girls talked well into the night. Tamara was reeling from the shock and couldn't believe that her father could do such a thing.

"Please, Aliya, let me call my father... I'm sure he can explain everything. Or, at least my mother."

"Not just yet. Not until we know for sure. Right now, I think Khalid is the only one who can help... but when I talk with him I will have to be careful," Aliya gathered up her things. "He could be involved as well but he's just recently returned from the U.S. and my father-in-law was complaining that he's been brainwashed by the Western ways." Aliya smiled reassuringly at Tamara. "I'm sure he wouldn't approve if he knew you were being kept under lock and key." She held up the key. "We can only hope he is not involved and can influence his father."

"Oh Aliya, I hope you're right... this is all so messed up," Tamara threw a pillow across the room. "And, it's not so much fun anymore either."

"I know but we're going to figure it out. I'm sorry I have to lock the door again but I'll be back in the morning to bring you breakfast."

"Why? How come I can't eat with you?"

"Things are really tense since we heard about Ali so I don't think it's a good idea for you to be in my father-in-law's sight. Don't worry, as soon as we finish breakfast I'll make an excuse to go out... Yusef doesn't mind me going on short errands without him as long as I'm covered. I'll tell them I need to go to the pharmacy for 'ladies' things. There's a huge one on the ground floor of Khalid's office building so my driver won't suspect anything. I'll go see him and then come back and fill you in, okay?"

"Okay," Tamara reached for Aliya and hugged her. "Thank you for helping me. I just want to go home."

# Chapter 30

Susan didn't need to see Celeste's red-rimmed eyes to know that it had been a rough night for her. The yelling and slamming of doors kept Susan awake until about three when it finally quieted down. She had started down the hallway at least a dozen times, worried the violence would escalate. At one point, she hovered outside the door for over an hour, but decided not to barge in only because Ryan had finally lowered his voice and Celeste's came across quiet but strong. She couldn't hear the whole conversation but the gist of it was Ryan lamb-basting her for embarrassing him in front of his bosses, berating her for being so 'weak', and insisting that Tamara didn't need her mother hounding her, especially with Celeste in such a 'state' and that she would see Tamara once they got back to Dubai.

"Hey Celeste… are you doing okay?" Susan walked around the kitchen island where Celeste sat perched on a stool with her hands wrapped around a mug of coffee and put her arm around her shoulder and squeezed. "Has Ryan gone to work?" She dropped her voice to a whisper.

"Yes, thank God," Celeste shook her head. "It was all I could do last night after he fell asleep not to take that brass and marble toilet paper holder to his head."

"Good thing you didn't," Susan reached for a mug and poured. "If we were in the States we could probably claim a crime of passion but here you'd be stoned to death in the town square."

"I know... I kept reminding myself that I had to hold my tongue and let him rant... actually I've been practicing that for years," Celeste said as the tears started welling up in her eyes. "I wanted to yell and scream that I knew he was a liar... that I knew Tamara wasn't in Dubai... that she was here," a sob escaped her lips. "I can't believe he would do anything to hurt her." She turned towards Susan, her eyes mirroring the tortured sorrow of a mother powerless to help her young.

"I know this is tough Celeste," Susan held her tight. "But, at least we can assume now that she's okay... you saw her last night. You've got to hold it together. Come on. We need to make a plan." Susan handed her a Kleenex and went to pour a glass of water and grabbed Celeste's medication from the counter. "Here take this... but only half a dose today."

"Okay... good idea. I don't want to be in a fog. Once we find Tamara and we can get out of here I'll be able to think more clearly... but, I've decided I'm going to leave Ryan. I'm going back home and Tamara and I will start a new life."

"One step at a time hon.... We *will* get Tamara and we *will* get out of here... don't you worry about that. And, after seeing Ryan's true colors and hearing some of the things he said to you last night I don't blame you one little bit. I could tell you were handling yourself and we had to keep things as normal as possible but I *so* wanted to bust through the door and put a stop to it. I can see now that he's a textbook bully and I have to tell you, you handled yourself really well. I'm proud of you."

"Thank you... I kept thinking of Tamara and it gave me strength," Celeste said and shook her head sadly. "I'm so tired of living in fear and I only just realized it since we've been here. I always thought it was me and my inability to handle the 'tough stuff'. That's what Donald always told me... said I was weak-willed and Ryan reinforced that notion after I married *him*."

Susan nodded but didn't say anything... encouraging Celeste to go on. Celeste was starting to purge and Susan was now firmly in the counselor's role.

"Even when I was growing up my dad used to tell me I needed to 'toughen up and grow a thick skin' if I wanted to make it in life. He even tossed me off a wharf one time before I knew how to swim. Said it was for my own good." Celeste took the half pill Susan handed her. "When Donald went missing, Ryan was right at my side... at first he made me feel safe. I let him seduce me when Donald had just gone missing. There had always been this sexual tension between us and I knew I didn't want to be married to Donald anymore. We had always been living in such back-water places I could never figure out how to leave," she paused and took another drink of water. "I didn't work, didn't have my own bank account, couldn't go out on my own... it was terrible. And, it only got worse after Donald was pronounced dead and I married Ryan... I was pregnant with Tamara... I knew she was Donald's but also thought I could convince Ryan she was his... " Celeste's voice trailed off. "I'm sorry to lay this all on you Susan. You must think I'm a terrible person. I just didn't know what else to do. It feels so good to finally tell someone." The tears were streaming unchecked down her cheeks now.

"Oh my God no... I think you've been in a very difficult situation; being mentally and emotionally abused for so long and now you're ready to fight back... and I'm here to help you."

"You barely know me... although you know me probably better than anyone else. I've never had any close girlfriends. I was always afraid to bring anyone home," Celeste looked down at her hands and sniffed and took a tissue from the box Susan pushed closer. "You got a lot more than you bargained for, didn't you? I'm sorry I've dragged you into the middle of all this... I'm sure this isn't what you thought was ahead when you befriended that sweaty lady from beach boot camp... another one of my failed attempts to 'toughen up' a bit." She chuckled and sighed. "But I am so grateful you're here with me."

"Well, don't give it a second thought," Susan waved her hand in the air. "Now, let's get some breakfast into us. We're going to need our energy today to put a plan in motion. Why don't you put some eggs on? Hopefully Ryan is going to be at the office all day."

"Yes, he even said he was going to be late and not to wait on him for dinner."

"Good... Now, I'm going to call Mitch and tell him what's going on and maybe he can get someone at the Saudi embassy in Dubai working for us from that end.

"No, no... you can't do that!" Celeste's eyes widened. "We don't know what's really going on here and what Ryan's done. God only knows who's involved. The more I think about it the more I think that guy who tried to run us off the road in Dubai was somehow part of this whole thing. Maybe he was supposed to grab Tamara then but when the police pulled up he couldn't complete the job."

"Okay, now you're talking crazy...," Susan re-filled her coffee mug. "But you might have a point. I guess we should be cautious. I still want to tell Mitch that we think we've found Tamara and we'll be coming home in a few days. Are you okay with that? At least he'll be expecting us and if anything goes sideways and we disappear or something, he'll report it to the police or the

249

American Embassy or something. He's already loaded for bear!"

"Okay, that's probably a good idea... but I don't even know what that means." Celeste wiped her cheeks and blew her nose.

"Sorry... guess you've been living away from the U.S. for too long... it just means he's spring-loaded and ready for action. He's sent a hundred text messages just checking in... I think he's anxious for me to come home. He said he didn't trust Ryan from the second he met him so he's nervous for you too."

"Well, it's good to know that there's someone out there who knows where we are and cares what happens. You're very lucky."

"Thanks... he's a real gem, for sure."

"Okay... so, go make your call and after you do, I think we should go talk to Karl."

"I think *I* should go talk to Karl... what if Ryan sees you?"

"He could easily see you too.... I say we go together... we can wear a full *hijab* so only our eyes are showing. Nobody will recognize us."

"I guess that makes sense. How will we get there?" Susan poured herself another coffee.

"Ryan drove himself today so we've got his driver at our disposal. I told him we had to get some groceries. There are hundreds of white SUV limos like it on the road and the windows are so darkly tinted no one can see inside. Ryan's working from the site now until the project is done so we shouldn't have to worry about running into him

250

but we won't uncover our faces until we're in Karl's office just in case. We should blend right in."

"Okay, so how do we get in to see him?"

"Well, it shouldn't be too difficult. You heard him say at the wedding that he'd like to catch up. It'll be a social call... like we're dropping by to see if he wants to go to lunch."

"Without Ryan? Isn't that 'forbidden'? Don't we have to be accompanied by a male relative?"

"Actually, if we were local women... unrelated to him that is... we'd never get away with it. But as American 'infidels' they almost expect us to flout the rules. But we're being respectful by covering so it shouldn't be a problem. And besides, as 'older women' it's not as big a deal."

"Okay. Sounds like we have a plan then... Let's get a move on."

## Chapter 31

Karl ran his hand across the stubble of his cheek and shook his head. For the third time, he flipped in disbelief through the papers that had come via courier that morning. He looked at the sender's name on the envelope again. It was from Ali. He shivered thinking about the dead man's message that had come too late for him. The realization that Ali probably hadn't taken his own life dawned as he slowly put the papers back in the envelope. He knew Ryan was a cold man... *but this?* He picked up his phone and punched his assistant's extension.

"Dahlia, please call my father's office and make an appointment for me to see him this afternoon... tell them it's urgent... thank-you." He could visit him at his home that evening but it couldn't wait. His father needed to know what Ryan was up to. What he had been up to for years if the documents in the package were authentic.

Karl's mind raced with incidents in the past where Ryan had shown serious unethical behavior. He remembered a time when Ryan had bought a research paper instead of writing it himself. But they were young and Karl had always put it down to immaturity. Ryan had gotten him out of a pretty big bind with the dean's daughter as well so he didn't think he could be too judgmental at the time. They were all young and ambitious and he hadn't given it a second thought. He hadn't seen Ryan at all after graduation, until recently when he became Ryan's boss, but bits and pieces were now making sense. Karl remembered a call he had gotten a few years back from a big conglomerate asking questions about Ryan and Rydo Construction, claiming they were looking for a reference. They asked a lot of strange questions that Karl couldn't answer. He said he hadn't seen or heard from Ryan in several years. They never called back.

Karl's intercom buzzed, bringing him back to the present. He pushed the speaker button, "Yes, Dahlia?"

"There's an Aliya bint Ahmed al Habtoor here to see you. She doesn't have an appointment but says it's urgent."

"Aliya? Of course, send her in."

Karl walked around to the front of his desk as Dahlia escorted his guest into the office.

"*As-Salaam-Alaikum*, Aliya." He put his hand on his heart and tipped his head slightly.

"*Wa Alaikum-As-Salaam*, Khalid," Aliya responded as she tucked her *shayla* more firmly under the tight fitting *niqab* underneath. "I'm so sorry to come unannounced."

"Not at all... you're family. You don't need an invitation. Please sit down," he pointed towards an armchair in the opposite corner of his office, next to a floor-to-ceiling window overlooking the city. "Would you like a coffee?"

"Oh, yes please," Aliya nodded. As she sat down Dahlia re-appeared as if by magic with a tray holding an Arabic coffee urn, two tiny coffee cups and a plate of sugar cookies and placed it on the coffee table in front of her. In the Arab culture one would never turn down an offer of refreshments, as it would be impolite.

Aliya fidgeted as Dahlia poured.

"Thank you Dahlia, that will be all," Karl took the cup that was handed to him and turned to face Aliya. "So, were you at the wedding party last night? I didn't see you."

"Yes, I was at the bride's party." Aliya nervously watched as Dahlia closed the door quietly behind her.

"That's right, of course... I did speak to Yusef briefly and he said you did the bride's henna."

"Uh... yes, I did."

"So, what brings you here today?"

"Well, I'm not really sure where to begin." The coffee cup rattled on the saucer in her shaking hands as she set it back down. "Actually, Yusef doesn't... and mustn't know I'm here." Aliya folded her hands on her lap to keep them from shaking. "Please... my father-in-law can't know I've come to see you either," she implored, folding and unfolding her hands.

"Why not? What is it Aliya?"

"I think they're holding a young woman against her will," she blurted out. "And, I think you know who she is... her father works for you... and, I think your father is involved," her hand flew to her mouth as if she had said too much.

"What are you talking about?" Karl leaned forward with his elbows on his knees and clasped his hands together as if in prayer. "Now, take a deep breath and start at the beginning. What makes you think that and why?"

Aliya did as he suggested and her jaw set in determination. "I know it's happening, but I don't know exactly why. I know because I've been 'entertaining' her. Her name is Tamara and she's Mr. Parker's daughter. You actually saw her briefly one day when you came to visit. She and I were coming down the stairs as you were coming in the foyer."

"Oh God... I remember her... I commented to Mohammed how beautiful she was," Karl got up and started pacing. "And, now that I think about it, she bears a striking resemblance to her mother. The same incredible blue eyes and silky blond hair." He looked at Aliya whose discomfort was growing. "I think I know why too." He glanced over at his desk where the courier package from Ali still lay. "Where is she now?"

"She's at our home... or, I mean the home of my father-in-law."

"Okay, I think I have a very good idea of what's happening here. Don't worry... I'll take care of it," Karl picked up the package and slid it into his briefcase. "You go back home and don't breathe a word of this to anyone. I won't tell your husband or your father-in-law you were here either."

"Thank you so much. I just have a terrible feeling that Tamara is in danger. I think her father's been embezzling and that she is being used to get back at him. And, when we heard about Ali's accident my father-in-law was enraged... I think he blames Mr. Parker."

"I think you're right. I received some information only this morning that could prove it. So, just go home, sit tight and wait until you hear from me. And, don't let Tamara out of your sight. If they want to take her somewhere tell them she's sick."

Just as the door closed behind Aliya, Karl's intercom buzzed again. He punched the speaker button. "Yes Dahlia, what is it? Did you get through to my father's office?"

"Yes, sir... he's expecting you in an hour."

"Thank you... Sorry, what did you need?

"You have visitors... They don't have an appointment and won't give their names. I told them you were in a meeting but they insisted on seeing you. Do you want me to tell them to make an appointment for another day?"

"No... That's fine. I'm curious... I'll come out. I guess my 'clear' calendar today was too good to be true."

Karl opened his office door and stepped in the reception area of his office suite. Two women fully covered in traditional Arab dress sat in the waiting area flipping absently through magazines. As he approached, both women looked up and he was immediately drawn to the mesmerizing set of cobalt blue eyes that stood out between the black swaths of fabric of the *hijab* that covered the rest of the face of the woman on the right.

"Celeste?"

Her eyes widened at his comment of recognition. She looked quickly over at his assistant who was busy speaking to someone on the phone.

"I'm so sorry to come unannounced but it's urgent I speak with you," she lowered her voice to a whisper. "Can we go somewhere we won't be overheard."

"Of course, please, come in." He showed the women into his office and turned to his assistant as she replaced the receiver on its cradle. "We won't be needing anything Dahlia... and please, no calls."

"Yes sir," she responded and turned back to answer another incoming call. As he closed the door he could hear her telling the caller that he was unavailable and could she take a message.

"Please make yourselves comfortable... would you like some coffee?" Karl indicated the coffee urn that was still on the table from Aliya's visit. He took two fresh cups from the trolley at the end of the couch and handed them to Celeste.

"Thank you," Celeste reached for the cups and placed them on the table and un-tucked the veil that covered her face from under her *niqab*.

"You remember my friend Susan from the wedding?"

"Yes, of course. Nice to see you again." Karl nodded his head and put his had to his heart.

Susan looked up from pouring the coffee and smiled. "I hope you don't mind me pouring. I'm dying for a cup." She handed one to Celeste who held her hand up.

"Not for me... I don't think I should be drinking coffee... my stomach's in knots."

"I think I know why you're here," Karl said softly and covered Celeste's hand in his.

"You do?" Celeste looked down at her hand but didn't make any attempt to move it. She looked up and her eyes filled with tears.

"It's about Tamara, right?"

Celeste pulled back and clutched at her hand like she had been stung. "Why do you say that?" She looked at Susan and back to Karl. "What do you know about Tamara?" Susan came and sat next to Celeste and put a protective arm around her.

"It's difficult to know where to start because there are still some unanswered questions."

"How about starting by telling me if you know where my daughter is?" Celeste's voice quivered but raised an octave. "Where is she Karl?"

"We know she's in Saudi," Susan interrupted. "Celeste is sure she saw her at the wedding... we came to ask for your help in finding her. She was kidnapped in Dubai and we believe she was brought here but we don't know why."

"Ryan's been behaving very strange and he's become violent," Celeste added. "I don't feel safe and I think Tamara's in danger."

"I think I can shed some light on this... and help you get Tamara back," said Karl.

"How," Celeste still looked suspicious but leaned forward intently.

"Well, I received a package today with some interesting documents and then had a surprise visitor who confirmed my suspicions. You're right to be worried. It appears that Ryan is involved but I don't want to say too much until I get a few more questions answered. And, at this point, the less you know, the safer you'll be. You're just going to have to trust me."

Celeste opened her mouth to reply but Karl's intercom buzzing cut her off before she could answer. He picked up the receiver. "Yes, Dahlia, I thought I told you I didn't want to be disturbed... Oh?... Okay, thank-you... yes, yes, you were right to interrupt. I do need to see him. Please take him to the small meeting room and give him some coffee and tell him I'll be right with him... oh, and call my father to let him know I'm running behind."

Karl hung up the receiver and turned slowly to face Celeste. "Ryan's here."

"What! Oh Jesus... he can't see us here," she fumbled with her headscarf, trying to twist it around her neck and tuck her hair in place.

"Don't worry... Dahlia will take him to another room and you and Susan can use my private elevator." He ushered them to an alcove at the back of his office and pushed the down button.

"But what if he saw our car and driver?"

"I'm sure he's parked way on the other end of the building. I saw a sign for VIP parking... I'm sure it's fine," Susan soothed.

"I believe Ryan does always park near the front entrance so there's no way he would have even driven past where the drivers wait," Karl reassured her. "Now go home and wait for my call. I promise I'll be in touch as soon as I can."

The elevator doors closed on his last words.

# Chapter 32

The apartment door swung open and Ryan stormed in startling Celeste and Susan out of their intense conversation. Celeste swallowed hard to still her thumping heart. She hoped he hadn't overheard anything.

"You're home? I wasn't expecting you," she started to stand up but her legs were shaking so bad she sat back down. "Do you have to go back to the office... can I make you some lunch?" she continued to babble, attempting to appear natural but feeling as though she was failing miserably. Surely he would suspect something was up. Susan started to help her gather their coffee mugs and napkins and Celeste could see her hands shaking as well.

"No, I'm not staying," he continued past them into the bedroom and barely looked at them. "I left some papers here I didn't think I'd need today," he re-appeared stuffing file folders in his computer bag. "They moved up the fucking walk through... was supposed to be next week but the Minister's coming himself and he'll be at the site in an hour and I'll have to show him the punch list." He stopped at the dining room table to re-arrange the contents of his bag so the files would fit. "I don't know what's at the office and what's at the site," he growled. "These people say jump and I'm supposed to say, how fuckin' high? God damned Karl, he's probably got something to do with this... he's pissed off about Ali and taking it out on me. After the walk through he wants to talk about whether or not we need a new project foreman at this late stage in the game."

"I can make you a quick sandwich to take with you if you like," Celeste offered half-heartedly, just wishing he would go.

"No Celeste... I don't want a *sandwich*... I'll have the driver stop on the way."

"Fine... I was just trying to be helpful," Celeste glared at him, a new feeling of anger bubbling up, giving her strength. She felt Susan's hand rest gently on her shoulder and she took a deep breath and bit her tongue to keep '*asshole*' from springing from her lips.

"Totally understandable," Susan directed a sympathetic nod towards Ryan. "I'm sure it's a bit stressful for you right now."

"You have no idea . . ." he shook his head. "I'll be taking the driver back so you guys will have to stay put. Probably best anyways. It's not a good idea for you to be out and about unaccompanied. Next time you want to go shopping I'll go with you."

"Don't worry, we can entertain ourselves, right Celeste?" Susan picked up the cups and walked into the kitchen.

"I'm sure you can," Ryan paused with his hand on the doorknob. "Actually Celeste, you should start making plans for Susan to head back to Dubai, don't you think? I'm sure her husband misses her. We'll talk about that when I get back later."

"But..."

He pulled the door open, stepped through and slammed it behind himself before she could reply.

Celeste slowly let out the breath she hadn't realized she had been holding. "Bastard," she hissed.

"Just wait until he finds out I'm not the only one going back to Dubai," Susan said. "We're going to find Tamara and the three of us will be going back. And, he'll have to deal with whatever mess he's created here."

"I really hope you're right," Celeste sighed and dropped onto the piano bench. "I wish Karl would call. Without his help we're royally screwed," she checked her phone again in case there was a missed call. "He should know something by now, shouldn't he? He seemed so certain. I can't stand this! My stomach is in knots! I've got to do something to find my daughter. I feel so helpless."

"I'm sure we'll hear from him soon," Susan said.

"I hope so," Celeste spun around to face the piano and started picking out the melody of 'Hall of the Mountain King.' As she progressed through a few bars she added her left hand bringing in the brazen footsteps of the trolls she pictured in her mind. She leaned into the chase at hand, swaying forward and back as her foot worked the pedal. As she reached the crescendo where she pictured an escape from danger and a daring rescue, there was a knock on the door.

Celeste jumped up and ran to the door almost knocking Susan over. She stopped short to check in the peephole and pulled the door open. "Karl! I'm so glad you're here," she stepped aside to let him in. "Did you see Ryan? He just left."

"I knew he was here because he told me he had to come get the documents for the inspection, so I waited down the street until I saw him leave."

"So it *was* you," Celeste genuinely smiled for the first time in a long while. "I can't tell you how much it means to me that you're helping find my daughter." She put her hand on his arm and looked up into his eyes.

"Celeste, I..." His voice trailed away and he pulled her into his arms.

She lost herself for a moment in the comforting embrace, the smell of Clive Christian cologne like aromatherapy. His arms tightened around her and she rested her head on his chest. She wanted to stay there forever and forget about everything. Then Tamara's face appeared in her mind's eye and she mentally shook herself and gently pushed him away.

"Tamara... Please Karl, tell me... where is she?"

He took a step back and then seemed to notice Susan for the first time since he entered the apartment. "Of course... hello Susan." He put his hand on his heart. "*A-Salaam- Alaikum*, so nice to see you again. Although I wish it was under more pleasant circumstances."

"It's nice to see you too," Susan motioned to the settee. "Won't you please sit down? I'll go ahead and make some more coffee. Looks like you might need some."

Karl nodded and lowered himself onto the coach. Celeste chose the armchair across from him not trusting what she now finally recognized as the all-too familiar draw she unavoidably felt when a 'big strong man' was there to rescue her. It was like an epiphany on a mountaintop. Until this moment, she had never considered herself needy and co-dependent. The sweet temptation to fall into his arms and let him take care of everything frightened her. *Can't I stand on my own two feet?* It was a question that would have to wait to be answered. This particular moment was not the time to 'roar'. They were in a tenuous situation in a male-dominated culture where her legal rights as a mother didn't matter, not to mention the fact that she suspected those who had Tamara were politically well connected.

Susan returned from the kitchen and put the tray of mugs, sugar and milk and a pitcher of water on the coffee table. "Coffee's brewing. It should only be a few minutes."

"Thank you Susan but I'm just going to have water for now," Celeste said as she turned to Karl. "Tell us what you've found out."

Karl took a deep breath. "This isn't going to be easy for you to hear Celeste."

"Is she okay?" She reached for Susan's hand and gripped it, preparing for the worst and felt a large lump lodge itself sideways in her throat, threatening to choke her.

"I'm sure she's fine but we have to act quickly and very carefully." He reached for one of the glasses of water Susan had poured, took a drink, swallowed and sighed deeply. "There's no easy way to break this to you Celeste so I'm just going to say it... Ryan has been embezzling from the company. In essence, that means he's been stealing from the Royal Family... my family. It looks like it's been going on for years. Not only with this project."

Celeste sunk back into the chair, dazed. "Are you sure? And, what does that have to do with Tamara?" She was trying to put all the muddled pieces together but the synapses of her brain weren't firing. She couldn't comprehend that Ryan would do anything to put them in danger.

"I'm just trying to put everything together too but as I understand it, my father discovered what Ryan was doing and took Tamara as a guarantee to get the money back."

"Oh my God," Celeste whispered and stifled a sob that threatened. "Took her where?"

"She's being held at my cousin's place here in the city but I'm assured she's being treated as a guest," Karl began. "After I saw you this morning, I confronted my father and showed him the package I told you about that I received today from Ali. In it were copies of bank statements from offshore accounts all over the world, holding millions of dollars. There was other incriminating evidence proving what Ryan was doing. My father had suspected something was up when one of the sub-contractors contacted him directly inquiring about his invoice. Ryan had been denying everything and claiming that all the expenses were legitimate. He's always been a charmer so I'm sure he thought he could talk his way out of it and have Tamara sent back to Dubai and nobody would be the wiser. But my father tapped Sheri, Ryan's assistant, to dig for more and she found some duplicate invoices that didn't match. I believe Ali found even more proof and probably tried to bribe Ryan."

"You think Ryan killed Ali?" Susan asked.

"It looks that way," Karl sighed again. "At first my father told me to mind my own business. He said that he was going to take care of both Ryan and his family."

"What?" Celeste sat forward again. "What did he mean?"

"That's not important," Karl leaned forward. "The main thing is that I convinced him you and Tamara were innocent in all this and that it would be cruel of him to make you pay for Ryan's mistakes."

"Karl, I need to see her," Celeste closed her eyes and put her hands to her face in a prayer. "Please." She was so exhausted and emotionally drained, her voice came out as a croak around the lump.

"I'll take you to her now," Karl replied. "Susan, I think you should come too."

"Just try to stop me!" Susan said. "And, just so you know, my husband knows exactly where I am. He works for Emirates and has a layover here in Riyadh tonight. He's expecting a call from me at his hotel when he arrives and will also be expecting to see me and Celeste tomorrow.

Karl laughed. "From the moment I met you Susan, I knew that Celeste had picked the right cohort," he turned to Celeste. "Please be assured, I'm on your side in this and won't let anything happen to you," he reached for her hand. "The Minister is going to meet Ryan at the site and then bring him to my cousin Mohammed's house for a 'follow-up' meeting. We'll be there waiting. If I have my way, you, Susan and Tamara will be on Susan's husband's flight headed back to Dubai tomorrow."

Celeste nodded, picked up her purse and headed for the door, feeling more than a little trepidation but threw her shoulders back in a posture meant to will more confidence than she actually felt.

Susan followed closely behind. "Well then, let's not waste any more time."

# *Chapter 33*

As they came up the half-kilometer driveway, pulled into to the circular drive and came to a smooth, rolling stop in front of Karl's cousin's house fear and uncertainty bubbled up like a blocked sewer overflowing in Celeste's gut. She wished the supple beige leather of Karl's gleaming white Rolls would swallow her up and transport her back to a time when life was simpler. Life before Donald and Ryan. Was she ever carefree? She couldn't remember. She dragged herself back to the present as Karl began to speak.

"Okay, we're going to go in now but please let me do the talking. I know you're anxious but the others aren't 100 percent convinced about what I'm proposing and we don't want to antagonize them. I need you both to understand that and keep covered at all times. I know it'll be tough but lower your eyes to show respect too, okay?"

"Respect!" Celeste spat out. "They've kidnapped my daughter and you want me to go in there demurely and bow down to them? They'll be lucky if I don't strangle them."

Susan put her hand on Celeste's knee to still her outburst. "Now that's the spirited gal I knew was in there... but it's probably best to just keep her under wraps for the time being. We're so close," she soothed.

"Susan's right," the pulse on Karl's neck was jumping. "If you don't keep it cool, I won't be able to control the situation."

"Okay, okay... I understand," Celeste took a deep breath in through her nostrils and exhaled slowly in an attempt to slow the pounding of her heart. She took another slow inhale and huffed it out through her mouth. "Okay, I'm ready."

They all exited the car and, with arms linked in solidarity, Susan and Celeste followed behind Karl. They stood on the lower step as Karl rang the bell, which they could hear reverberate through the foyer. Before the chimes were even finished a tall, African butler opened the huge oak door.

"We're here to see Mr. Mohammed," Karl said and the butler motioned them to come inside.

As they entered the cavernous vestibule Celeste glanced up to see a lovely young Saudi woman with kind eyes gliding down circular stairway as if on air, her *abaya* floated around her ankles obscuring her feet, completing the illusion.

"*As-Salaam-Alaikam*, Aliya," Karl acknowledged her. "May I introduce you to Celeste, Tamara's mother, and her friend Susan."

"*Wa-Alaikum-As-Salaam*, Karl," she smiled nervously and turned to Celeste and Susan. "Welcome to our home."

"Thank-you," Celeste clenched her fists inside her sleeves and forced a smile.

"Ms. Celeste, I am sure you're anxious to see Tamara and she's equally as excited to see you."

"She knows I'm coming?" Celeste unclenched her hands.

"Yes, she does. If you'll please come with me, I will take you to her." She held out her arm and guided Celeste to the staircase then turned to her maid who had followed quietly behind. "Sasha, will you please show Ms. Susan to the ladies' *majlis*?"

"Yes, Madame," the maid turned to Susan. "This way please."

Celeste reached and grasped Susan's hand.

"Celeste, it's going to be fine," Susan gave her a squeeze. "I'll see you and Tamara real soon." She turned and followed the maid down a long corridor off the foyer.

Aliya turned to Karl as Celeste hovered at the foot of the stairs. "My father-in-law is in the main *majlis* waiting for you. The Minister is not here yet but is expected to arrive any minute with Mr. Ryan. I should get Ms. Celeste out of sight. Fahad will show you in," she nodded at a gentleman dressed in a chauffeur's uniform.

"Thank-you Aliya for all your help," Karl said.

"Don't thank me yet," she paused. "How do you say it? We're still in the woods."

"Don't worry, I can see daylight through the leaves," Karl said, then turned to follow Fahad as Aliya led Celeste up the staircase.

Celeste couldn't keep the tears from streaming down her face as she was led down a thick red, richly carpeted hallway. The thought of seeing Tamara and the relief from knowing that she was okay flooded all her senses. Through her tears she could see the walls were lined with portraits of an assortment of powerful looking men. They all wore white robes covered in flowing black silk cloaks, adorned with gold clasps and intricate embroidery as well as the traditional white or red and white checked headgear, known as a *ghutra*, with a black rope or *agal* circling the crown of the head to keep it on. She recognized one as King Abdullah, the Saudi ruler. She had seen his face on billboards placed in high traffic areas throughout the Kingdom. She wondered how close the family tie to the King actually was as a shiver started at the base of her spine and crept its way up to the back of her neck, making the fine hairs stand up on end.

"Aliya, what are you doing? Who is this?" a young man came up from behind.

"Yusef, where have you been? I've been waiting for you. Have you spoken with your father?"

"No, I haven't since breakfast, why?" He looked at Celeste curiously. "*As-Salaam-Alaikum,*

I'm Yusef, Aliya's husband," he said as he started wringing his hands and shuffling from one foot to the other. Celeste noted that his greeting wasn't arrogant, just curious. He was actually quite polite... almost humble.

"I'm so sorry... Yusef, this is Tamara's mother, Celeste. I'm taking her to see her."

"Oh, Aliya! What have you done? Father will be so angry. I knew you were getting too attached." He turned to Celeste. "I'm sorry but you must go before it's too late." He started pushing Celeste back the way she came. Celeste side-stepped him and circled around to stand behind Aliya, shooting him a fierce look that only a mother being kept from her child could muster.

"No, Yusef, it's okay," Aliya put her hand on his chest, blocking him from Celeste. "Karl's here and the Minister is coming. Everything's going to be fine and Tamara will be going home with her mother. He promised. But, you must go now and tell them you agree with Karl; that Mr. Ryan is the only one who should be punished. You and I both know it's the truth and Karl says he has convinced the Minister but we have to convince your father now... as well as Fahad," her voice faded as Yusef shook his head.

"Fahad wants blood," he said sadly. "It's more than just the money now. He wants to avenge his brother's death."

"Yusef, we're all devastated about Ali," Aliya said softly. "But, that still doesn't change the facts and you have to help him understand that the old

273

ways are out-dated. He trusts you and will listen to you. They're in the *majlis* now waiting for you. Please Yusef... try... for me?"

"Alright my darling, I'll do my best."

She stood on tiptoes and kissed his cheek and turned back to Celeste. "Come on then. Tamara's waiting."

As they continued down the corridor it seemed never-ending and Celeste thought of the movie The Green Mile. She now knew how those men felt although she hoped that Karl's plea was successful and, unlike the death-row inmates, she, Susan and Tamara would all get out of this with their lives. She cursed Ryan under her breath. How could he be so callous? Her mind raced with all the signs she had chosen to ignore. She finally realized that the wounds of his childhood ran much deeper than he would admit or that she had been willing to recognize in his intense behavior over the years. But, it didn't matter how or why. She could never forgive him for this.

Aliya stopped at the last door at the end facing them and took out a key. Celeste's breath caught in her throat with the realization that Tamara was locked in - a prisoner. No matter how well she had been treated, she was still trapped like an animal. No matter how gilded the cage was she hadn't been allowed to come and go freely.

"Mom!" Tamara came flying across the room and practically bowled her over as she threw her arms around her mother's neck and clung to her. "I'm so glad you're here," her voice was muffled in Celeste's hair. "I missed you."

"I missed you too sweetheart," Celeste inhaled the sweet scent of her daughter and held her tight. The weeks of stress and fear melted away as she held Tamara at arm's length, scrutinizing every inch to make sure she was whole and unharmed. She pulled her back into a bear hug. "I'm so glad you're okay."

"I'm okay mom," Tamara pulled away and looked over at her friend. "Aliya and her family have been keeping me safe. But, what the hell's going on with dad? Aliya says he's in trouble. That they think he's been stealing from the 'Family'... but I can't believe it. It's not true, right?"

Celeste glanced at Aliya and with her arm around Tamara's shoulder guided her to the couch. "I'm not sure... what else did Aliya tell you?" Celeste raised her eyebrows at Aliya.

"Tamara knows that her life was in danger but I wasn't able to give her many details. I told her you would explain," offered Aliya.

"Explain?" Celeste turned to Tamara who was looking at her expectantly. "I'm really not sure where to begin..." she paused, then took a deep breath. "I don't understand it entirely myself, but I'll try."

Karl willed his hand to stop shaking as he poured a coffee and handed it to his cousin. "I'm glad you feel the same way I do." He stole a glance at Fahad who stood scowling in the corner. Yusef hovered protectively close by.

"I don't entirely agree but I am a reasonable man," Mohammed accepted the cup that Karl held out. "I can see the conflict you are feeling... but I also see your loyalty to family so I am willing to compromise and let the women go. And, I'm sure Fahad will come around." He turned to his chauffeur and inclined his head.

"Thank you Mohammed," Karl put his hand to his heart and turned to Fahad. "And your brother's killer will pay. I'm sure the authorities will want to talk to Ryan now that this new information has surfaced."

"Let us wait and see what the Minister has in mind," Mohammed sneered. "He may have other plans for our friend *Mr.* Ryan... however, according to our laws, murder is punishable by death... or, have you forgotten?"

"No, I haven't forgotten," Karl stood up and began pacing. "If he did kill Ali, then he should be held responsible. If the courts find him guilty, Fahad will be given the opportunity to insist on the death penalty or accept compensation."

"Yes, that is true," Mohammad smoothed a non-existent crease from the starched white fabric of his *dish dasha*. "Either way, Fahad will have his revenge."

"Excuse me sir," Aliya's maid, Sasha, hovered in the doorway. "The Minister and Mr. Ryan are here.

"Well, bring them in then," Mohammed waved his hand.

Karl paced another length of the room and then positioned himself at the entrance to the salon, bracing himself for the confrontation that was imminent. He adjusted his tie as his father's imposing figure filled the doorway. It just didn't matter how old he was, how educated and responsible he had become, his father's presence always sent a chill up his spine. Karl had seen how ruthless he could be but hoped their discussion that morning and his agreement with Karl's plea to spare Celeste and Tamara would hold. Hot bile rose in his throat as he fought back his doubts about his father's ability to empathize with the women's plight. He desperately hoped that his position as the eldest male of the family would carry enough weight to soften his father's fierce loyalty to the old traditions.

"Ah, my cousin," Bashir stretched his arms wide in greeting to his host. "*As-Salaam-Alaikum…* Thank you for allowing us to conduct our meeting in your glorious home." He firmly grasped Mohammad by both shoulders and planted a kiss on each cheek.

Mohammad returned the gesture and stepped back smiling widely. "*Wa-Alaikum As-Salaam.* You are always welcome in my home."

"Karl, *As-Salaam-Alaikum*," Bashir repeated the grand, cheek-kissing gesture with his son and then turned back to Mohammad.

"I believe you have met Mr. Ryan Parker, the gentleman who is building the King's Community and Convention Centre."

"Yes, we met at the wedding... *As-Salaam-Alaikum* Mr. Ryan."

Ryan stepped out from behind the Minister and, placed his hand on his heart and bowed. "*Wa-Alaikum-As-Salaam*," Ryan replied then dropped his hand to his side, both fists clenched. "Hello Karl," his eyes narrowed to slits. "I wasn't expecting to see you here."

"*As-Salaam-Alaikim*, Ryan," Karl smiled stiffly. "I wanted to hear how the walk through went and, we have other business to discuss as well."

"We do?" Ryan looked around at the others. "Yes, I suppose everyone is eager to hear about plans for the grand opening," he rushed ahead. "I know Miriam and Sheri have been putting the guest list together and are waiting for word that we'll be finished on time... I assured the Minister that we will - even with Ali's untimely death. The men are working double overtime and I'm on site every day to make sure they don't slack off."

Yusef stepped forward leaving Fahad standing as stiff as a sentry, obviously seething inside, glaring with unmasked hatred at Ryan.

"Please everyone, come sit, have coffee," Yusef motioned for the butler, who was standing motionless in the corner, to pour.

Once each of them was seated with cup in hand, the Minister began. "Well, I'm very pleased with the status of the project and Ryan has certainly kept everything on target," he paused and raised his cup in a toast. The others followed suit. "We were fortunate to see the final installation of the Chihuly in the main entry-way... spectacular piece." He took a sip, placed his cup on the small, low table on his right and leaned back on his elbow, propped on a red and gold bolster.

"I'm glad you're pleased..." Ryan began but Bashir raised his hand, silencing him.

"I wouldn't say 'pleased' is the right word," he said as he studied the tassel on the end of the clasp that fastened his *bisht*. "More like disgusted. Or, maybe dismayed." He shook his head.

"I beg your pardon?" Ryan sat up.

"Yes, you will... but I'm not sure I can give it."

"I'm not sure I understand. As I showed you, everything is done... only some minor finishing details to go like the gold faucets in the VIP boxes, which will arrive tomorrow and be installed before the end of the week."

"Ah yes, the gold faucets. I'm glad you brought those up." He held out his hand. "Karl, I believe you might have the invoices for those."

"Yes, I do," Karl handed a file folder to his father.

"Why do you have those?" Ryan swallowed. "Can I see?"

"In a minute," Bashir began. "But, first I have a question." He pulled a sheet of paper out of the file and held it up. "This purchase order for $2.8 million from Goldwerks was submitted by you for these faucets and paid into the Rydo Construction account, correct?"

"May I see it, please," Ryan repeated and the Minister handed over the piece of paper. It fluttered as Ryan held it, seeming to study the contents. "Yes, I believe you're right."

"Okay... then, what is this?" Bashir held up another sheet of paper. "It's a purchase order with the same number from the same company, but it's for less than half the amount."

Karl watched intently as a drop of sweat sprouted out from Ryan's furrowed brow and ran down the side of his face.

"Sir, I can explain..."

"I hope you can. I thought during our last conversation you said there were a 'few' discrepancies that you would take care of. There is more information that has come to light that causes me great concern. I haven't had you arrested because you're worth more to me alive than dead. But, I can't say the same for your lovely wife and daughter."

Ryan wiped the sweat bead that dangled from his chin as several more formed on his forehead. "What information sir? As for these invoices, if I recall correctly, they made a mistake

280

on that first purchase order and only included half the amount we needed." He handed the paper back. "It's just a clerical error. I promise you."

"Well, that will be easy enough to prove," Bashir held his cup out and the butler floated silently over, re-filled it and retreated to the corner. "And, coincidentally, a very interesting package arrived at Karl's office by courier this morning," he held out his hand as Karl handed him a thick envelope. He pulled out a stack of papers and began handing them one by one to Ryan.

"What are these?" Ryan flipped through each one as the color drained from his face.

"Well, the first several appear to be copies from two sets of books from Rydo Construction, that go back several years," Bashir paused and let Ryan get through the stack. "The next batch are duplicate invoices but with different amounts. We've been suspicious for a while, which is why we had Ali watching you for the past several months."

Bashir paused to allow Ryan to process the information. Everyone in the room had grown silent and Fahad's expression and posture had become even more menacing.

"There was still the question of what you had done with all the money," Karl stepped forward. "But, this file that was also in the courier package helped fill in the rest of the details." He handed over a file folder. "My guess is you were getting overconfident and got sloppy. These are statements from numbered accounts in Singapore and Zurich."

"I've never seen these before in my life," Ryan stammered weakly as he sifted through the documents.

"That's funny because there was a note in the package as well... from Ali before he was murdered."

"Murdered? But I thought the police determined it was suicide?" Ryan stood up and started slowly backing up towards the door. Fahad moved quickly behind to block any possibility of an exit.

"Oh, Ryan, have you met Ali's brother, Fahad? He's very curious to find out exactly what you might know about Ali's 'suicide'. Would you like me to read what was probably the last thing he wrote before he died?"

Without waiting, Karl unfolded a piece of paper and began to read:

*Dear Khalid,*

*If you are reading this, I'm afraid I might have met with an unfortunate end. This package was left with a friend who had instructions to courier it to you in the event of my death. Your father has documentation that led us to believe that Mr. Ryan has been embezzling from the company. This package contains additional documents that go back several years as well as bank statements that I found in Mr. Ryan's office during his recent trip to Dubai, further proof of his deep deceit and disloyalty. I send this to you as I understand that because of what he's done, Mr. Ryan's family could be in danger and I wish them no harm...*

"I don't need to continue... you get the idea."

"Loyalty?" Ryan spat. "Ali was trying to use this to bribe me and extort money... he's not the martyr you think he is... he was playing both sides. If I had agreed to his demands you never would have gotten these..." his breath was cut off as Fahad's arm encircled his neck from behind.

"You will not speak ill of the dead in my home!" Mohammad advanced on Ryan but the Minister raised his hand.

"Please cousin," he began. "Remember, we have a plan... a proposal.

Mohammad backed away and nodded to Fahad to release his nemesis. Ryan coughed and rubbed his neck.

"Mr. Parker, you have two options."

"Yeah, what are they?" Ryan straightened his collar and scowled at Fahad.

"Well, we could hand you over to the authorities and then wash our hands of you," he paused and took a sip of his coffee and sat back. "Or, you will continue to work for us, until your debt is paid. We will pay you the regular contract rate but will keep the majority of it and allow you enough to feed and cloth yourself. We will hold your passport and you will sign over access to your offshore accounts and we will take possession and recover the money you stole and pay Fahad the 'blood money' for his brother Ali's death. We will provide 'housing' on whatever construction site you happen to be working on at the time. Once the debt is paid, we will determine at that time whether or not you will be allowed to leave the Kingdom."

"But, that could take years," said Ryan as he dropped down onto a cushion, with his head in his hands.

"Yes, it will... but if you choose your first option and you're found guilty of murder, you'll be be-headed for your crime, which I believe Fahad would prefer," Bashir looked over at Fahad who inclined his head ever so slightly. "But we've convinced him that he should waive his right to see you die and to take the money instead. At the moment I'm feeling generous and will allow you to make the choice."

# *Chapter 34*

Celeste gently wiped the tears from Tamara's cheeks as Aliya passed them a box of Kleenex.

"But mom, I don't understand," Tamara blew her nose as more tears filled her reddened eyes. "Why would daddy do such horrible things?"

"I don't really know sweetheart," Celeste sighed. "He's been under a lot of stress lately..." her voice trailed off realizing how lame an excuse that sounded. Tamara would eventually have to be told the truth about her real father and what happened to Ryan as a child, but now wasn't the right time. Her main concern was getting both herself and her daughter out of the country.

There was a knock on the door and Aliya opened it a crack. She had a rushed, whispered conversation with Yusef, quietly closed it again and turned to Celeste and Tamara.

"My father-in-law would like you to come and say good bye to Mr. Ryan. Karl will then take you to the airport. A private jet is waiting to take you back to Dubai," Aliya reached for Tamara's hand. "Come, I'll help you pack your things."

"But I thought that we would just join Susan's husband's flight in the morning," Celeste started gathering the contents of her purse she had dumped while looking for a tissue. She could feel her heart starting to race. "Susan and I still have our things at the apartment." Her hand closed around a prescription bottle of Xanax. She shook one out and glanced at Tamara. She looked away as she popped it in her mouth and took a drink of water.

"We've already taken care of that and your suitcases are in the car waiting for you," Aliya reached for the Louis Vuitton carry-on she had given Tamara. "Please, come now. The sooner you go the better... before the Minister changes his mind."

"Ok... but Tamara can wait here," Celeste said firmly.

"No Mom, I'm not a child any more," she put her hands on her hips. "I need to see him, look him in the eye and ask him why."

Celeste shook her head. "I don't think it's a good idea. There's nothing he could possibly say to make it any better."

"Mom... please! I want to see him."

"Okay," Celeste gathered her daughter into her arms and gave her a squeeze. "Let's go then." The calming effects of the pill started to kick in. It was the extra help she needed to hold it all together, and there was no shame in that. It was better than having another meltdown right now.

They hurried down the hallway and down the winding staircase as Celeste held Tamara's hand in a vice grip the whole way. She wasn't sure she'd ever let it go again. They stopped briefly at the ladies *majlis* and motioned for Susan, who wordlessly joined them. She must have been briefed already, Celeste thought as their entourage came to a halt in front of the closed double doors of the main salon. Celeste's heart was in her throat. She had no idea what or who she was about to face. Ryan's multiple personalities came on at the most unexpected moments and could switch in a split second. In this extremely stressful situation, there was no telling which one was behind that door. He had never been clinically diagnosed but Celeste now knew in her heart that she wasn't the only one suffering from a mental illness. The only difference was she had admitted to hers and was seeking help.

Yusef reached out for the doorknob, paused and looked back at Celeste and raised his eyebrows. She nodded and clenched her teeth. She was as ready as she would ever be. Susan squeezed her shoulder and Celeste was reassured that her friend had her back.

Yusef and Aliya entered the room first and Celeste, Tamara and Susan followed closely behind. It was the final act. Celeste's entire body vibrated from emotion as she entered from stage left and took in the scene around her. She was flanked by the butler who had let them in, on one side, and the chauffeur she had seen earlier on the other. His face was etched with a furious frown but the butler seemed more bewildered, his eyes darting from person to person, waiting for his next order.

She looked further into the room and recognized the Minister from his portrait in the hallway. In real life he was ominous. His huge, black-cloaked frame loomed over a crumpled male form on a cushion in the circle of the *majlis*. The man had his head in his hands. He looked disheveled, pathetic and frightened.

As the newcomers entered the room, the man raised his head. Celeste gasped. It was Ryan! She almost ran to him to comfort him but as she watched, Ryan's look of surprise turned to sheer hatred. It was the punch in the gut she needed to solidify her resolve. Why hadn't she seen it before... probably because she had been so passive and always did what she was told. No more! She stepped in front of Tamara and folded her arms across her chest as Susan came up to stand beside her, blocking Tamara from his view.

"What the hell are they doing here?" Ryan drew himself to his feet and glared at the Minister.

"They are here to say good bye," Karl stepped between Ryan and the women.

"The hell they are," Ryan advanced on Karl like a snarling dog. Fahad sprinted from his post at the door and covered the 20 feet in a split second, moving at lightening speed for a man of his size, and tackled Ryan to the ground. For the second time that afternoon he encircled his enemy's throat with his massive hands.

"Enough!" the Minister yelled. "Fahad, release Mr. Ryan." Fahad did as he was told and yanked Ryan to his feet but still held him in an arm-lock.

"Celeste can go but Tamara will stay with *me*," Ryan spat out between heavy breaths and coughing.

"Over my dead body," Celeste reached behind her to make sure Tamara was still there and looked up at Karl. He gave her elbow a squeeze.

"Ryan, I don't think you are in any position to make demands. We've already explained what your options are and they don't include having either your wife or daughter remain behind with you."

"You bastard! You've always had a thing for Celeste, haven't you?" Ryan stopped struggling and shook his head. "Well, you can have her," his shoulders drooped and the fight seemed to drain out of his body.

"You don't know what you're talking about," Karl's voice came out measured and controlled. "Fahad, please take Mr. Ryan to the study and we'll be right there."

"Mr. Ryan, take some time to think about our offer," the Minister added. "It won't last long. Before you leave this house, you need to decide. You either return to the site and continue your work, or we turn you over to the authorities."

Still holding him in an arm-lock, Fahad pushed Ryan towards the door.

"Dad?" Tamara's one word hovered in the air as Celeste's heart broke for her.

Ryan stopped and turned, "I am sorry honey... I didn't mean for any of this to happen." His voice trailed away as Fahad continued to push him out the door and out of their lives.

"Now, for you ladies," the Minister began.

"Father," Karl interrupted. "You don't need to worry about them. Arrangements are made to take them back to Dubai tonight. I will escort them to the airport myself and make sure they board the plane."

"Fine," the Minister waved a hand. "I don't want to think about this any more. I have more important matters to attend to. Just take care of it."

# Chapter 35

As they pulled up to the private jet Susan let out a squeal. "Karl, you didn't tell me that Mitch would be here." She jumped out of the car and ran into her husband's waiting arms.

"Tamara, why don't you go ahead and get on the plane with Susan and Mitch." Celeste had finally let go of her hand once they got into the limo at Mohammad's. "I'll be right there."

"Okay... I'll save you a seat," Tamara attempted a smile but Celeste saw her chin quiver. It was going to take a while for them both to heal but they would be all right. They had each other. The thought fortified Celeste like a bowl of soothing chicken soup. A flood of relief washed over her as she watched out the tinted windows as Mitch, Susan and Tamara boarded the plane. The captain and flight attendant remained at the foot of the stairs to wait for their last passenger. She knew, because of the darkly smoked glass, that she could see them but they couldn't see her.

"Karl, I can't thank you enough for all you've done," the tears started welling up in her eyes. She had fought them back to be strong for Tamara but she couldn't hold them back any more. Karl gathered her in his arms and she sobbed into his shoulder. He stroked her hair and murmured comforting words. Celeste wanted to stay wrapped in his cocoon of safety forever but collected herself and pulled away, wiping her stained cheeks.

"Celeste, you don't have to thank me," Karl smiled. "I'm just happy that you and Tamara are safe." He took a deep breath and continued. "There was one thing that Ryan said that was true though."

"Oh, and what was that," Celeste busied herself combing her hair and looking at herself in an ornate compact she had pulled out of her purse.

"I have been in love with you since the day we met," he took her hand in his. "I could come to Dubai with you..." he didn't finish.

"I had no idea," Celeste pulled her hand away. "I won't lie to you, I have felt something between us but you were Donald's best friend and then Ryan's boss. I just thought it was a physical attraction so I ignored it."

"Well, you don't have to ignore it anymore, if you don't want to."

"Karl... there's just too much I'm dealing with right now," Celeste pleaded with her eyes for him to understand. "I made the mistake of running into another man's arms before when things were crashing down around me. At the time it seemed like the only solution." She paused. "This time, I have to heal myself and take care of my daughter... I hope you understand."

"Of course I do," Karl smiled. "Another time and another place. Maybe when you can trust again."

"Yeah, maybe." Celeste fiddled with the clasp on her purse, afraid to look into his eyes again.

"I almost forgot... here, you might need this."

"Oh?" Celeste reached for the envelope Karl held out and shook out the contents. "Jesus, it's Tamara's passport. Where did you get this?" The hair stood up on the back of her neck as the image of her daughter's open night table drawer popped into her head.

"Mohammed had it," Karl held up his hand as Celeste opened her mouth to talk. "Don't ask... it's better you don't know. But, promise me you'll find somewhere else to stay when you get back to Dubai."

"Okay." She fingered the blue-covered document.

"So, no more, questions. And, when you go, don't ever look back." Karl started fidgeting with his sleeve and moved to the far side of the back seat. "Celeste, there's something else I have to tell you because I think it might help with letting go... but it's not going to be easy to hear."

"I don't know if I can take any more but you might as well go ahead," she said with a forced laugh.

"I honestly had my suspicions about Ryan a long time ago, even when we were at school

293

together," he paused. "Then when Donald went missing..." he stopped and bit his upper lip.

"Go on Karl, you can't stop now."

"Well, when I got the news of Donald's disappearance, things didn't really add up but then you married Ryan so I made myself forget about it. I didn't want to add to your stress." He took a drink from a water bottle out of the limo's mini-bar and put the cap back on. Celeste waited quietly for him to continue. "A few months later I got an unusual call from one of the companies in Lagos Ryan and Donald were doing work for. They asked a lot of questions about my involvement with Rydo Construction. At the time, Ryan was pitching another project in The Kingdom and I wasn't involved, so I really couldn't offer much insight. Putting all the pieces together, I couldn't help but think that Ryan had something to do with Donald's disappearance. I think Donald knew Ryan was embezzling money even back then and confronted him. I don't have any proof of this, but thought you needed to know."

"Jesus," Celeste started hyperventilating and leaned forward to put her head between her knees as Susan had taught her.

"I'm so sorry Celeste," Karl rubbed her back. "Maybe I shouldn't have said anything.

"No, I think I needed to know," her voice was muffled as she stayed in her doubled over position. "Just give me a minute." She stared at the floor and tried to absorb what Karl had said as more tears filled her eyes, rolled down her nose, and dripped onto the toes of her shoes. After the past few weeks, she marveled that there were any left. Her whole marriage had been one lie after another. Yet another kick in the gut. The realization that the man she had spent the last 19 years with was not only a crook but possibly a murderer as well was a lot to process and it wasn't going to happen overnight. She stayed hanging over her knees as she felt a wave of nausea rise in her throat. She swallowed and successfully fought it back. She remained that way for a while and Karl stayed silent.

Finally, she sat up and smoothed her hair down again. She looked over at the plane and saw Tamara poke her head out of the door and wave for her to come.

"Right then, I think I'd better go," Celeste sniffed and straightened her *abaya*. "They're going to think you've spirited me away."

"I really wish I could," Karl said. "But, I understand you need to work this out for yourself. But, if you ever need anything, I'm just a phone call away."

Celeste leaned over and kissed him on both cheeks, picked up her purse and got out of the car. She threw her shoulders back and walked towards the plane and didn't look back once.

# # #

*Anne Louise O'Connell*

## ABOUT THE AUTHOR

Anne Louise O'Connell grew up in Halifax, Nova Scotia and has been an expat since 1993 when she and her husband escaped the cold of Canada on a hunt for warmer climes, with stops in Florida, Dubai and Thailand. In 2007, after almost 20 years in the PR business, O'Connell decided to focus on her real passion and just write. O'Connell is a multi-genre author having written three other books prior to *Deep Deceit*. She authored *@Home in Dubai... Getting Connected Online and on the Ground*; *10 Steps to a Successful PR Campaign-A Do-it-Yourself Guide for Authors*; and *Mental Pause*, her first novel that won a bronze medal in the 2013 Independent Publisher Book Awards (IPPY). She also recently co-published an anthology titled *Phuket Island Writers – An Anthology of Short Stories*. Now that her second novel has launched she's convinced that fiction is her 'new calling'. She is currently working on her next novel, *Deep Freeze (the next in the Susan Morris Expat Mystery series)* and is also in the process of adapting *Mental Pause* into a screenplay.

O'Connell mentors other authors, does developmental editing and assists others in developing their author platforms. She enjoys editing women's fiction, memoirs and sometimes children's books so she can return to her roots as a preschool teacher. She is a contributing writer for Wall St. Journal Expat, Expat Focus and Global Living Magazine. In her 'spare' time she loves beach combing, traveling, reading, volunteering, mentoring, walking, swimming, writing and yoga.

Connect with Anne:

Website: www.annelouiseoconnell.com
Blog: www.anne-writingjustbecause.blogspot.com
Twitter: @annethewriter
Facebook: www.facebook.com/annethewriter
LinkedIn: www.linkedin.com/in/anneoconnell

If you'd like updates from the author on book launches, events, writing retreats and workshops, sign up for her newsletter at:
www.globalwritingsolutions.com/Newsletter_Sign-Up.html

*Anne Louise O'Connell*

Other books by Anne Louise O'Connell:

Mental Pause
www.mentalpause-thenovel.blogspot.com

@Home in Dubai – Getting Connected Online and on the Ground
www.athomeindubai-gettingconnected.com

10 Steps to a Successful PR Campaign – A Do-it-Yourself Guide for Authors

*All available on Amazon on print and on Kindle.

Or, you can buy a signed PDF copy available at:

Books by Anne Louise O'Connell
http://shop.globalwritingsolutions.com/

*Deep Deceit*

Made in the USA
Charleston, SC
06 March 2016